The Hunting Season

www.rbooks.co.uk

Also by Dean Vincent Carter:

The Hand of the Devil

DEAN VINCENT CARTER

CARTER

The Hunting Season

CORGI BOOKS

THE HUNTING SEASON
A CORGI BOOK 978 0 552 55298 1

First published in Great Britain by The Bodley Head,
an imprint of Random House Children's Books
A Random House Group Company

The Bodley Head edition published 2007
Corgi edition published 2008

1 3 5 7 9 10 8 6 4 2

The Random House Group Limited supports the Forest Stewardship Council (FSC), the leading
international forest certification organization. All our titles that are printed on Greenpeace-approved
FSC-certified paper carry the FSC logo. Our paper procurement policy can be found at
www.rbooks.co.uk/environment

Mixed Sources
Product group from well-managed
forests and other controlled sources
www.fsc.org Cert no. TT-COC-2139
FSC © 1996 Forest Stewardship Council

Corgi Books are published by Random House Children's Books,
61–63 Uxbridge Road, London W5 5SA

www.kidsatrandomhouse.co.uk
www.rbooks.co.uk

Addresses for companies within The Random House Group Limited can be found at:
www.randomhouse.co.uk/offices.htm

THE RANDOM HOUSE GROUP Limited Reg. No. 954009

A CIP catalogue record for this book is available from the British Library.

Printed in the UK by CPI Bookmarque, Croydon, CR0 4TD

For Mum, Dad and Darryl.
And for Charlie, for making a dream come true.

'... And when there are two in one blood and in one soul, who are at deadly enmity, then life fares ill'

Herman Hesse, *Steppenwolf*

'Man is the cruellest animal'

Friedrich Nietzsche, *Thus Spoke Zarathustra*

1: THE CREATURE CREEPS

Talbot sighed like a deflating football.

'What's the matter?' Evans asked as she overtook an elderly man in a battered three-wheeled car. It was already dark but at least the rain was abating now. Ahead of them the traffic lights turned to red.

'Nothing,' Talbot replied. 'I just . . . It'd be nice to actually see something – you know, before I get reassigned.'

The lights changed to green. Evans accelerated away.

'I presume by "something" you mean the supernatural. And you're not going to be reassigned. Not for a while anyway.'

'We'll see.' Talbot yawned. Evans glanced across and laughed. 'What?' He squinted in confusion. 'What's so amusing?'

'Nothing. It's just that we've got a potential lycanthrope on our hands here and you've got the nerve to yawn.'

'Yeah, well, I bet it turns out to be nothing again. Just a big bloody dog – it'd be great if it really was a werewolf though.'

'I'm not sure "great" is the word I'd use. And without wanting to sound pedantic, I think it's a wulver we're after rather than a werewolf.'

'Remind me of the difference.'

'OK, remember Lon Chaney Junior and Oliver Reed in those old werewolf movies?'

'Yeah.'

'Well, back then it was easier to glue hair onto an actor's face and shove some plastic fangs into his mouth, so they ignored the original definition of a werewolf. A werewolf is a man who turns into wolf – completely.' She dropped down a gear and turned left into a residential street. 'A wulver, fully transformed, is half man, half wolf, like what you see in most so-called "werewolf" movies.'

'Right, so werewolves aren't meant to walk around on two feet when they've changed – they're just . . . wolves.'

'Well, bigger, meaner and hungrier, in most cases – but yes, when transformed they're wolves. Two legs wulver, four legs werewolf. Easy to remember.'

'And what we're after today is a wulver.'

'I reckon so. But don't worry about classification too much. If you want to call it a werewolf, that's fine with me.'

Evans pulled up outside a small semi-detached house and glanced at the adhesive note she'd stuck to the middle of the steering wheel. 'Number nineteen should be a couple of houses up. Are you ready?'

'Yup,' Talbot said, unbuckling his seat belt. 'By the way, why do you pretend to be a regular constable? I mean, you're a detective inspector – wouldn't you like people to know that?'

'To be honest I'm not bothered. I only mention it when I need to. The job's the important thing, not the title.'

'Spoken like a true professional,' Talbot said, stepping out of the car and slamming his door shut.

It didn't take them long to find the house. They knocked on the door and waited. Seconds later a small, balding man appeared and let them in. His skin was pale and he looked shaken.

'Please, this way. My wife is in the living room. We tried to get the neighbours to help us, but they just looked at us as if we were mad – oh, it's so terrible,' he went on, his voice shaking. 'I'm still not sure what I saw, but it wasn't normal.'

'No,' Talbot said, glancing at Evans. 'Well, hopefully we'll be able to help shed some light on the matter.' The assumption remained that this would turn out to be another disappointment.

They were led into the living room, where they found a small woman clutching a cup of tea and looking like she'd received the fright of her life.

'Mrs Goddard?'

'Yes,' she replied, almost spilling the tea in her shaking hands as she looked up.

'I'm Janice Evans. I work with the Metropolitan Police.'

'Oh . . . I thought you *were* the police.'

'Well, we are and we aren't,' Talbot said, smiling.

'We're a special division,' Evans said, turning to Talbot and giving him a disapproving glance. 'We employ police officers *and* civilians, all experienced in unusual cases. This is my partner, Kevin Talbot.'

'Oh, thank you both so much for coming,' Mrs Goddard said. 'Please get rid of it. It's . . . horrible.' She put her mug down on the table in front of her and stood up. 'It was out there.' She pointed towards the back garden. The curtains had been drawn across the patio doors. Talbot looked from Mr to Mrs Goddard and saw that neither were in any hurry to pull the curtains back.

'What exactly did you see, Mrs Goddard?'

'It was ... it was like a big dog. But it was walking upright like a man, and it was wearing clothes.' She started wringing her hands together. 'Can you believe that? I thought it was someone dressed up, but then I heard Ted coming downstairs and it ran off down the garden faster than anything I've ever seen,' she said, looking Evans in the eye. 'I swear to you – it couldn't have been human.'

'OK,' Evans said, placing a hand on Mrs Goddard's arm. 'If it's still out there we'll find it. And we'll make sure it can't harm you.' She looked at Talbot, who nodded, though he was wondering how exactly they would provide the protection Evans promised. That's if there really was something outside.

He walked across the living room and slowly moved one curtain aside. Despite his scepticism he half expected to see something jump out in front of him. Then he cursed himself for being stupid. He had to get close to the glass to be able to see past the light reflected from the living room, but even then he couldn't see anything out there in the gloom.

'Well,' he said, drawing the curtains back all the way and gripping the handle of one of the doors. 'Best take a look.'

While Mr and Mrs Goddard waited in the living room, the two officers from the Department of Unexplained Crime walked out into the garden with only the light from the house to illuminate their surroundings. The garden was big. The patio ended a couple of metres from the house, where it met the huge lawn. Halfway down on the left was a greenhouse, and at the far end was a large shed, with trees behind it. There could have been something down there, but from this distance it was impossible to tell. Evans looked at her partner, waiting for him to take the lead. He smiled in return, noting how apprehensive she looked.

'If there's anything there, it's probably just some kid,' he said.

'"Some kid"? Trust me, it's never just "some kid".' She took a few deep breaths. 'Well, off you go.' She gestured towards the other end of the garden with one hand.

Talbot accepted the invitation and walked along the patio, then onto the grass. They both pulled out medium-sized, slimline torches and began shining them into the bushes and flowerbeds along the garden's perimeter. They were directing the beams towards the greenhouse when a noise interrupted the quiet. It was Evans's mobile phone.

'Typical. Excuse me.' She unclipped the phone from her belt and pushed a button. 'Hello? Yeah . . . Yeah, no problem . . . Look, I'll call you from a land line, OK? This battery's nearly dead.' She pushed another button and replaced the phone. 'Sorry, Kev, I've got to call the office. I'll see if I can use the phone in the house. Don't go any further, OK? Wait for me to get back.'

'No probs – I'll just hang out here for a while,' he said, frowning.

'I won't be long, I promise. Ah, here you go,' she said, seeing Mr Goddard approaching from the patio. 'He'll keep you company.'

'Thanks.' Talbot waited as Evans exchanged a few words with Goddard. Then she went into the house and the man approached him.

'I think it must have gone over there,' Goddard said, pointing towards the shed. 'There's trees behind there it could hide in.'

'Mm,' Talbot replied, shining the torch in that direction. 'Well, we should really wait for my partner to get back, but . . . that thing must be long gone by now. No harm in us taking a quick peek.'

'Do you want me to go and get a knife from the kitchen?'

'What for?'

'You know . . .' Goddard said, making a stabbing gesture with his right hand.

'No, no, that's OK,' Talbot replied, embarrassed. 'I'm sure we'll be fine.'

They approached the small wooden shed, split up and circled it until they met round the back. The trees in front of the wall at the back of the property were dense, even though they'd lost their leaves. It was too dark to see everything there: the beam from the torch didn't seem to penetrate much more than a metre.

'Mr Goddard, I think you and your wife can relax. Whoever was here is long gone by now,' said Talbot.

The two men walked back round to the lawn and turned their backs on the shed.

'So . . . so what do you think it was?' Goddard asked.

'Well, don't tell my partner I said this, but it's probably just some kid messing around. Some of them get a thrill out of running through other people's gardens – seeing how many they can get across before they're caught. Or it could just be a student prank.'

'Students?'

'Yeah. You know what they get up to.'

'Oh,' Goddard replied doubtfully.

As they were passing the greenhouse on their right, Talbot stopped. A strange feeling came over him. Turning round, he looked back in the direction of the trees. Nothing. Goddard continued towards the house, oblivious. Talbot turned back, then thought he heard a sound from the direction of the greenhouse. Looking through the glass, he saw that it contained only tomato plants, empty fertilizer bags, large plastic trays, plant pots and . . . two bright yellow orbs, like small, boiling suns. They were behind the greenhouse, up against the fence, and though they were filtered through the two layers of thick, grimy glass, their ferocity was awesome. Talbot moaned as the eyes began to move, then started backing away towards the house.

'What's wrong?' It was Goddard. 'Is it . . . ?' Then he must have seen what Talbot had, as he cried out and ran back across the patio to the house.

'Get inside,' Talbot screamed. 'Now!'

The beast came round the greenhouse and emerged into full view.

'Oh Christ,' Talbot whimpered in a voice not his own, as the monstrosity rose above him, opening its jaws wide. The eyes, the amazing, burning eyes, were the last thing he knew.

2: THE DEATH SEASON

'What's your name, love?'

'Gerontius Moore.'

'Sorry?'

'Gerontius – G-E-R-O-N-T-I-U-S – Moore.'

'Oh, right. That's a lovely name.'

'Yeah . . . I mean, thanks.'

'And what can I do for you, Gerontius?'

'Well, I've brought the form in for the trip. Mr Baring said I could drop it in to reception during the holiday.'

'OK – have your parents signed it? We'll need their signatures, of course, for the—'

'Um, no, they're dead.'

'Oh . . . oh, I'm so sorry, sweetheart.'

'That's all right.'

'Have you had it signed by your legal guardian?'

'No, not yet.'

'Who is your legal guardian?'

'Well, I live with my aunt and uncle.'

'I see, and can they do it?'

'Er, they're not home at the moment.'

'Ah.'

'They should be back tomorrow though.'

'All right then, if you can ask them to sign the form here, where indicated, and bring it back tomorrow, or Friday . . . Is that going to be all right?'

'Um, yeah.'

'Good, because Friday's the deadline, you know. Sorry if it means you have to make a special trip. I bet you'd rather be enjoying half term, wouldn't you?'

'Yeah. It's OK though. Thanks.'

'You're welcome. Take care now.'

'I will. Thanks very much.'

'Bye.'

Outside the administration building, Gerontius stood scanning the nearly empty car park. He'd wasted at least an hour bringing in the form for the trip. He'd hoped that being an orphan would make him exempt from needing signatures. And anyway, it was only a few days in Paris – what the hell was the consent for? He ran a hand through his brown hair that really needed cutting, and headed towards the road. The sky was clear and the sun was strong, even for autumn. With nothing else to do, he could have a nice relaxing day. He decided to catch a bus to the mini-market to see his cousin. No doubt she'd want to moan at him about working during half term. He couldn't believe she was that desperate for money. He turned right and walked down the road towards the bus stop.

When the bus arrived, Gerontius boarded and found a window seat near the front. It wasn't long before tiredness overcame him. The low drone of the engine, the motion of the vehicle and the warm sunlight on his face only increased the drowsiness. His eyelids tripled in weight, and slid inevitably down over his eyes, plunging him, with a jolt, into sleep . . .

Austria
Eight years ago

'Oh, it smells good here,' came his father's voice. There was a sound of rushing air. He must have opened the window again. The temperature inside the car was dropping already. 'Can you smell that pine? Wow.'

'Oh, for heaven's sake, close that window, it's freezing!' his mother snapped.

'They call them *hamrammrs* in Iceland – werewolves, I mean.'

Gerontius wasn't sure if his father had actually said these words, or if his memory had somehow distorted them. But the dream always began that way.

'So what?' His mother's voice again. Self-assured and playful. 'We're in Austria, not Iceland.'

'I know, I just like the sound of that word. *Hamrammrs . . .*'

'I wish that old man had kept his stories to himself.'

'Oh, he was only winding us up. Probably sick of tourists driving through here upsetting the peace and quiet.'

'I didn't know we *were* upsetting the peace and quiet.'

'Well, someone's got to,' he said, grinning.

'You're driving on the wrong side again, honey.'

'Oops.' He swerved back over to the right side of the road. 'Sorry, it's hard not to keep moving back over.'

'I'll forgive you.' Nadia Moore brushed a lock of brown hair away from her face as she looked out of the window to her left. 'He did seem pretty serious though . . .'

'Oh, don't worry. If we come across any monsters I'll just drive over them.' Harry Moore reached forward and turned on the radio. Almost immediately his head started bobbing as the rock music took over the vehicle.

'Turn that down, you'll wake him!' Nadia whispered sharply. She turned round to look at the young boy curled up on the back seat, his eyes blinking open.

'Aw – did your nasty dad wake you up, sweetie?'

'Ungh.' Gerontius sat up slowly and looked out of the car window.

'He'll miss the whole bloody holiday at this rate!'

'No he won't – he's just not used to all this travelling.'

'Well, he'll have to get used to it sooner or later.' Harry Moore looked at Gerontius in the rear-view mirror. 'He'll be driving us around one day . . . or driving us around the bend.' He chuckled and looked back at the road.

Gerontius watched the endless forest roll past, snow blanketing everything but the branch tips. *What's in there?* he thought, rubbing his eyes. *What exactly is in an Austrian forest?* He was bored. That was the main reason he'd fallen asleep. His parents had given him a guide book to read, but that was like seeing his boredom written down on paper in more elaborate detail. He was sick of being driven from one obscure town to the next. He was sick of learning about *architecture* and *culture*. He wanted to enjoy himself. That was what a holiday was all about. His parents were enjoying themselves, but that only made the situation more infuriating. He ached at the thought that he could be at home in his nice warm room watching TV or playing computer games. That sounded like fun, certainly more fun than holidaying with Mum.

Ahead of them the road turned sharply to the left. Harry stopped moving to the music to focus on the bend. The road was icy and uneven. Losing concentration here could lead to trouble. Gerontius half hoped the car would spin out. At least then there'd be some excitement. They slowed as Harry changed down into second gear. Nadia chewed her bottom lip and stared through the windscreen. The bend was tighter than she'd first thought. The road just disappeared. Gerontius sat forward, his head between his parents' seats, to get a better view.

'Hey, you! Sit back and put your seat belt on. How many times—?'

'But it digs in—'

'Now!' Harry barked.

'Oh . . .' He slumped back in his seat and fastened his belt. This, it seemed, was going to be the general theme of the holiday. Now he wished he'd caught the flu and been forced to stay at home.

The car continued to slow, then Harry began steering it round the bend. Gerontius could feel the back tyres resisting, as though they wanted to fly to the right and turn the car round, but despite the slippery surface, they kept their grip. His father pushed once more on the accelerator and took the car on to the next straight section of road. They began to pick up speed again.

'Phew,' he said, glancing across at his wife. 'I could do without challenges like that.'

'Keep your eyes on the road!' As she too looked back at the road, she saw something huge leap out from nowhere, land on the bonnet of the car with a loud bang and bounce off into the bushes to their left. Harry hit the brakes. The car stopped.

Gerontius had only had a brief glimpse of the thing that had struck the car, but it had been huge and had looked like no animal he'd come across before. It actually looked like something he'd seen in a film once, but that was . . . ridiculous! He watched his parents turn to each other, mouths gaping.

'What the hell . . . ?'

'Let's get out of here, Harry.'

'But we hit something.'

'Did you see it?'

'Yeah.'

'So did I, and I don't want to wait around for it to come back. Come on!' Terror warped Nadia's features.

Harry hit the accelerator hard, the tyres spinning wildly, and the car leaped forward.

'Mum,' Gerontius began, 'what *was* that?'

'Shh, sweetheart, it was nothing.'

Bang. This time it landed on the bonnet and stayed there, gripping the metal frame around the windscreen, glaring first at the driver, then at the passenger. Nadia and Gerontius screamed at the sight of the thing before them, while Harry lost control of the car.

They jerked in their seats as they swerved over to the left. Gerontius could see the hill sloping down to the valley below. He prayed his father could get the vehicle back under control and stop them going over the edge. Harry wrestled with the steering wheel, but the icy road was having its own way. Gerontius could now only gawp at the creature on the front of the car. It was big and covered in grey and white fur, with a mouth full of long, cruel teeth. The head was like that of a wolf, but the body . . . wasn't. As it growled and glared at them, it pulled back one clenched fist, then slammed it into the windscreen, shattering it and almost punching a hole straight through.

With gritted teeth, Harry Moore put all his strength into trying to regain control of his car while Nadia mouthed *Oh God, oh God* over and over again. Gerontius saw the creature let go of the car and fly backwards into midair, a split second before the car left the road. He could feel the left side of the vehicle dig into the ground while the right side lifted up and began to turn over. It all happened so fast.

They started rolling down the hill, Nadia screaming every time her side of the car slammed into the ground. Loose objects were thrown around them. The bonnet sprang up, then banged back into place. Harry's door also flew open to slam once more into its frame. Glass shattered, panels buckled. The world spun – endlessly, it seemed – until with a sound like the felling of a tree, the car landed on its roof for the last time, rocking slightly from side to side. There was a hissing noise, the sound of wheels spinning madly, then everything went black.

Gerontius opened his eyes eight years later and tried to dispel his disorientation. He looked frantically through the window, trying to process what he saw as the bus pulled away from the stop. *Damn!* It was *his* stop. He leaped up and darted to the front of the bus, pleading with the driver to stop. The man cast him a quick glance of annoyance, then halted the vehicle, opening the doors without a word. Gerontius called out his sincere thanks, even as he jumped through the doors and down onto the pavement. Ahead of him, further down the road, was the stop where he could catch the second bus he needed, and to add to his bad luck, there was one about to pull away. He swore and took off towards it, hoping the driver would see him in the mirror and wait. The bus, thankfully, remained where it was, but just as he was about to reach the door, his foot caught on something on the pavement, he was thrown forward and his right elbow scraped against the surface of the rough pavement.

Swearing didn't help, but it couldn't be avoided. Even with the protection of the sweatshirt he was wearing, the injury had still drawn blood. He could see the red staining the material already. He got to his feet, winced at the pain, then climbed onto the bus to face the staring driver. He rolled up one sleeve to look at the wound. The woman saw the blood and reached into her pocket. As Gerontius swiped his travel card across the electronic reader, the driver handed him a wad of tissues.

'Here you are, love. Are you all right?'

'Oh, thank you. Yeah, I'll be fine. Just wasn't looking where I was going.'

'The speed you were going, I thought something was chasing you.' She gave him a sympathetic smile, then turned back to the road, ready to move off.

Gerontius smiled back and took a nearby empty seat, dabbing the wound with the tissues that had already soaked up much of the blood. The positive side of the injury, he realized with little enthusiasm, was that he was unlikely to fall asleep again.

The sky had turned grey. If it rained, his sweatshirt wouldn't offer much protection. Shepherd's Bush was only a few stops along though. Hopefully he would stay dry until he reached the shop where Leah was working. It was owned by his Aunt Alison and Uncle Colin, who were spending a couple of days in Brighton to celebrate their wedding anniversary. He looked around the bus. People were casting him glances as he dabbed at his bleeding elbow. Feeling suddenly self-conscious, he rolled his sleeve back down, stuffed the wad of tissues in his pocket and closed his eyes, pretending to sleep.

Eyes. Yellow eyes. Insane, hungry . . .

He jumped in his seat. It was as though the dream hadn't gone, but was still lurking beneath his consciousness, waiting for him to weaken for just a second. The bus was approaching the stop he wanted. He jabbed the red button on the handrail in front of him; the bus slowed, stopped, and the door opened with a prolonged hiss. He stepped down onto the pavement and looked around. Al's Express Mart was only a few buildings along.

As Gerontius entered the shop, he saw that Leah's strawberry-blonde hair was tied back in a ponytail and she was wearing the neon-pink trainers that he found so disgusting.

'Hope you're having a better half term than me so far. How did you get on?' she asked as Gerontius closed the door behind him, one hand pressing the wad of tissues against his wound again.

As Leah noticed the large red stain, her expression changed to one of alarm. 'Bloody hell, what have you done?' She moved out from behind the counter and took hold of his arm so she could see the damage.

'I tripped on the pavement running after the bus.'

'Ow – I bet it kills.'

'Yeah, it does.'

'Hang on, I'll get Hortense to watch the shop so we can go out the back and get the first-aid kit. Hortense!' Leah's call was answered shortly afterwards by a middle-aged Jamaican lady who had been in the middle of a stocktake.

'There's no need to make a fuss,' Gerontius protested.

'Yes there is. I've done a first-aid course, remember.'

'Oh, right,' he replied sarcastically.

'What's wrong?' Hortense asked from further down the shop.

'Gerry's hurt himself. I need to take him out the back to get a bandage or something.'

'Yeah? What's he done?'

'Nothing,' Gerontius said, feeling that too much fuss had already been made. 'It's just a scratch.'

'Scratch?' The woman's eyes rolled as she caught sight of his arm. 'You look like you been fighting with a tiger or something. Go on, go and get it seen to, young man.'

Leah set to work on the grazed elbow straight away. She took a bottle of Devoida disinfectant from a cupboard below the sink in the small kitchen area, then retrieved the dusty green box with the white cross on it from a cupboard nearby. She first rinsed her cousin's wound with water, then with a good measure of the strong-smelling anti-bacterial formula.

'God, that stuff stinks!'

'Shhh.' She kept dabbing at the raw flesh until the pain finally kicked in.

'Ahh!' He flinched, knocking Leah's arm and pouring nearly half the bottle's contents all over his arm.

'Oh, you idiot,' she scolded. 'Now look what you've done.'

'You shouldn't have used so much. It's burning!'

'You big baby.'

'Shut up.'

'You shut up! Look at this mess.'

Grabbing a few sheets of kitchen towel, the two of them set to work cleaning up the spillage on the floor. The smell was overpowering. Gerontius washed his arm in the sink twice with hot soapy water, but the pungent aroma was going nowhere. For the time being he would have to live with it. Hearing the commotion, Hortense called out from the front of the shop.

'We're fine,' they both answered.

Once the elbow was dry, Leah dressed it with a bandage and gave her cousin a grin. 'Now be careful next time.'

'Thanks,' Gerontius replied, feeling slightly embarrassed.

They walked back into the shop and allowed Hortense to get on with her stocktaking. Leah hoisted herself up onto the stool behind the counter, and they both looked out of the shop window.

'Saw a dead dog on the way here this morning,' Leah said sadly.

'Where?'

'By the park. Looked a mess. Must have been in a fight. There was an RSPCA guy there though, so . . .'

'Oh, right.'

'You know, I don't like autumn.'

'What? Since when?'

'Since someone told me it was bad.'

'Bad?' Gerontius grinned, testing the bandage on his elbow to see how much the wound hurt. He winced.

'Yeah, bad things happen in autumn. It's the death season.'

'The *death season*? What the hell does that mean? I bet it was Mandy who told you that. You shouldn't listen to her new-age mumbo-jumbo.'

Gerontius felt annoyance – and a little anger – as he remembered that it was during the autumn that his parents had been taken from him.

'Mm. Maybe,' Leah replied. 'Do you want some orange juice?'

'Yeah, please.' Gerontius leaned against the counter, looking up at the TV mounted in the corner opposite. 'It's nearly half one, you know.'

'So?' Leah asked as she took a small carton of juice from a chilled cabinet next to the counter.

'*Brainbox* is on.'

'Oh yeah, I forgot.' She handed him the carton, then reached for the remote control and switched on the TV.

As *Brainbox*'s opening credits began, Gerontius heard an odd buzzing noise. Looking down at his feet, he saw a wasp with its legs in the air, kicking madly. After a few seconds of animation it stopped and lay still. Maybe autumn *was* the death season.

3: LITTLE PIGS

During the night rain had laminated the drive of the scrap yard with a coating of shiny leaves. When the three men finally showed up, twenty-five minutes late, they were laughing and joking, unaware that the worst day of their lives had begun.

Cain, a tall, confident black guy, rarely seen without his sunglasses regardless of the weather or season, was laughing his trademark laugh. Bale, his younger friend, was sharing the joke, much to the annoyance of the third, older, man, Mason. As the two men playfully exchanged the odd punch and kick, Mason wondered yet again why they couldn't behave like professionals, or at the very least act their age. He shook his head. He was always professional. He took the work he was given seriously. That was the only way to do it. Messing about led to mistakes. Sometimes fatal mistakes. He turned to look at his associates, both still smirking. Sometimes, when they were concentrating and not fooling around, they could be useful. Perhaps they were just bored. They would be working again soon though. That would give them focus.

'All right, lads, that's enough,' Mason said. 'Get it together.'

'Bloody hell!' Cain exclaimed. 'If you've got dirt on the

back of these . . .' He was trying to examine the back of his trousers where Bale had kicked him. 'Idiot,' he said.

'Why don't you give some cash to your poor old mum occasionally, instead of squandering it on clothes?' Bale asked, grinning.

'My mum's fine, don't you worry. She'd want me to look after myself.'

'Yeah, well, you're doing a great job of that.' Bale ducked to avoid another slap.

They approached the small portakabin at the end of the path through the scrap. It was a drab, featureless site. Maybe this was why the boss had chosen it. Inconspicuous, out of the way. Mason walked up and knocked three times on the door. Nothing. The boss was making them wait. This didn't surprise him. It often happened when they were late. He'd have to knock again.

'What are we waiting for?' Cain had stepped up next to Mason, practically breathing over his shoulder.

Mason knocked again. 'Manners,' he replied. They waited a few more seconds, then entered.

The cabin's internal lighting was very rarely used – the daylight that streamed through the two windows was usually the only source of illumination. This made it shadowy and uninviting. Today there was additional light from a small bar heater to the left of the only desk, which at that moment was unoccupied.

'Where is he then?' Cain sounded irritated.

'He's probably round the back with Benny.' Mason turned and stepped down from the cabin, followed by the other two. They walked round the back into a large open area surrounded on three sides by huge walls of wrecked cars and scrap. In the middle of the yard Slaughter, a short but intimidating guy, balding, scarred and with a couple of days' stubble growth, was puffing on a cigar and talking to another man about a car parked nearby. As the three men approached, Slaughter was becoming animated, pointing at the boot of the car with his cigar.

'Just crush the bloody thing, for crying out loud. Leave everything else to me.'

'But it's the smell, boss. Last time it reeked for a bloody fortnight. Got into me clothes and every—' Benny Fraser suddenly noticed the trio and fell silent.

'Listen, Smashy,' Slaughter said, using the man's nickname, while jabbing a finger into his chest. 'I don't give two shits about the bleeding smell. I just want it crushed and dumped.' He turned and saw the three men. 'Oh, it's you lot. 'Bout fuckin' time! Haven't you three got watches?'

'Yeah, sorry we're late, Ray,' Mason said. 'Traffic.'

'Traffic, my arse. Now go and wait inside. I've got to finish educating Smashy here on efficient waste disposal.'

'Come on,' Mason said to his colleagues. 'Let's go and make ourselves comfortable.'

'Not too comfortable,' Slaughter called after them. 'You're late already.'

Mason sat on the small padded chair near Slaughter's desk. Cain and Bale took the two less comfortable plastic chairs behind him. Bale fidgeted. Cain looked around the small cabin, then scratched his head.

Mason was still feeling apprehensive. Slaughter was often in a foul mood, but something was different today. And he hardly ever shouted at Benny. They were friends from a long way back.

'Hey, Mason,' Cain said, leaning forward and speaking into the older man's left ear. 'What's got the boss man spooked? He's not still miffed about the—?'

Footsteps and a plume of cigar smoke at the door signalled Slaughter's presence.

'You're late,' he reminded them. The voice was deep, roughened by decades of dedicated smoking.

'Yeah, sorry, Ray,' Mason said sincerely. 'There were hold-ups.'

'Really? That's a shame. Because if you'd been here on time I'd have had a really nice job for you. As it is' – he blew out more smoke and crushed the cigar butt into the ashtray – 'I gave it to Magnus.'

At this Cain and Bale moaned in unison.

'He gets all the cushy jobs,' Cain whined.

'Yeah, he does,' Slaughter said, glaring at the younger man. 'Because he gets here on time.' He scribbled something on a piece of paper in front of him, then sat back, twirling a ballpoint pen in the fingers of his right hand. 'Luckily for you three, I have another job that needs taking care of.' He made eye contact with each of them to make sure he had their complete attention. 'I want you to run a little errand for me. A nephew of mine bought an old theatre in Shepherd's Bush a couple of weeks ago. It's a bit of a dump and he was going to renovate it, but he's not going to have the time now.'

'Why's that?' Cain asked. 'He lose interest?'

'Nah,' Slaughter replied without changing expression. 'He's been arrested. But I want you three to go over there and sort through his office. He's a dopey little sod – that's why he was caught – and I want you to make sure he hasn't left anything behind that could put me in a delicate position. Understand?'

'Sure,' Mason said. 'But how do you know the police haven't been there already?'

'I've got a friend in the Met. He's managed to buy me a little time – only a day or two though. That's why I want you guys to go in and clean up before my time runs out.'

'What sort of stuff are we looking for?' Bale sat forward, interested.

'Anything. Any bit of paper you find, I want.'

'I understand,' Mason said. 'No problem, Ray.'

'Right then, off you go. The power's still on in there so you won't need torches. Just don't make too much noise or draw attention to yourselves.'

'Is that it then?' Mason looked a little confused.

'Yeah.' Slaughter nodded. 'That's it.'

'Don't you want us to burn the place or anything?'

'No. I don't want any attention drawn to it. All right? Just get in and out without anyone seeing you.'

'OK,' Mason conceded.

Slaughter looked back at his desk now. He seemed eager to conclude business. 'Here's the address.' He held out a small piece of notepaper.

Mason stood up, took the note and scanned the writing. 'What do you want us to do afterwards?'

'Afterwards?' Slaughter grinned. 'Just come straight back here with everything you find. I'll want to go through it. All right?'

'Right.' Mason looked down at the note again.

Cain and Bale stood and turned towards the door.

'I'll meet you outside,' Mason told them. When the door had closed he gave Slaughter a concerned look. 'Ray . . . this is a pretty strange job.'

'Strange?' The boss looked confused. 'What do you mean?'

'Well, it's not the sort of thing we're used to. We're . . .' Mason sat down again. 'Look, this isn't because of the Knightsbridge thing, is it? Like I said, we weren't used to handling such a huge place. There were more people than—'

'Ralph . . .' Slaughter said, looking him in the eye.

'Please, Ray. I want to sort this out. You know we're good blokes. We've done some pretty big jobs for you in the past. We're a solid crew. Those two lark about a bit, but they know their stuff. They're smart. You know that. We deserve a second chance, but . . . this job – it's just a bloody clean-up. I used to do these when I started out. This ain't right. We shouldn't be doing this.'

'Look, we've been over this, my friend.' Slaughter was trying to stay calm.

'I know, Ray, but it's like you're punishing us.'

'I told you not to worry about that foul-up. Mistakes

will be made. At the end of the day, you weren't caught. The police can't trace the crime back to me. That's the important thing. Like you said yourself – these things happen. We live and learn, my friend. And for God's sake, relax – you're heading for a heart attack. I should know – I've had three of them.' He chuckled and shook his head.

Mason's expression hadn't changed, however. 'So there's no hard feelings?'

'Of course not. Now go on, get out of my sight.'

Mason nodded and stood up. He folded the small piece of paper and put it in his pocket. Looking at his watch, he said, 'So . . . we'll be back here about four – OK?'

'Mmm?' The boss looked up. He hadn't been paying complete attention. 'Oh, uh, yeah. Fine. Oh, and Ralph . . .'

'Yeah?'

'You'll be needing this.' Slaughter produced a small brass key from his pocket. 'For the front doors.'

'Thanks. Well, see you in a while then.' Mason reached for the door handle, cast one last look at his boss, then left the cabin.

'I very much doubt it,' Slaughter said to himself.

Outside, Cain and Bale were already halfway down the path. They stopped and waited for Mason to catch up.

'What was all that about? You took your time,' Cain said.

'Nothing – just seems like a strange job, that's all.'

'It's because we messed up Knightsbridge, isn't it?'

'No,' Mason said, fixing Bale with a firm look. 'It's not that. Well, sort of.'

'Ah, this ain't right, mate.' Cain shook his head. 'It wasn't our fault. It was a big bank.'

'Yeah, there were too many of them in there,' Bale agreed.

'Yeah.' Mason turned and shot a glance back at the cabin. 'I know.'

As they left the scrap yard and turned down Garnier Road, a figure that had been waiting behind a wrecked minibus emerged onto the leaf-strewn path and walked casually towards the portakabin. He knocked three times on the door as Mason had done, then waited.

'What is it now, Ralph? I'm a busy man.'

The door opened and the visitor stepped inside, sniffing the room as he did so.

'Oh, are you Granger's mate?' Slaughter said, before looking at his watch. 'You're early. I thought you said you'd be here at two-thirty.' He reached into his top desk drawer and pulled out another cigar, which he lit.

'I did,' his visitor said, sitting down in the chair by the desk. 'But I wanted to get a good look at them.'

'You're lucky you didn't bloody bump into them. They should have left here half an hour ago.' Slaughter felt nervous. He'd only spoken to the man on the phone before, and the voice alone had been enough to give him the creeps. But now that he was here in person, there was an over-whelming sense of menace. The man was tall, broad, and wore clothes that seemed at least a size too large for him. He had his fair share of scars too. But these things alone weren't enough to make an impression on someone like

Slaughter. It was the eyes. They weren't normal. Every now and again when the man moved, the light seemed to catch something within, creating an unusual shine.

'So, you've made up your mind then?' Slaughter asked.

'I have,' the visitor replied. 'Have you?'

'Of course. I want them killed like I said. All three of them.' Slaughter dragged deeply on the cigar, keeping the smoke inside for longer than usual before expelling it. 'You've got the go-ahead.'

'Good.' The visitor stood.

'They'll be going to the theatre I mentioned before, the Emperor in Shepherd's Bush. It's disused. Everything's boarded up except the main entrance. Here . . .' Slaughter held out a couple of keys. 'The doors are locked now – but just with one key, which Mason has. I've given you the key to the second lock, which you can use once you have them inside.'

'Fine.' He took the keys from Slaughter's hand.

'They messed up one of the biggest, best-planned jobs I've ever done. They lost me a fortune. I'm feeling very vindictive right now. So by all means, do this in whatever way you like – just make sure they die.'

The visitor nodded, but didn't smile. 'About collecting the money – do you want me to bring some proof, or is my word good enough?'

'Proof?'

'Yeah, like a part of them.'

'Jesus, no,' Slaughter said, screwing up his face. 'I'll take your word for it.'

'Right.' With that, the man rose to his feet, turned and walked over to the door. 'See you later then.'

'Hang on . . .'

'Mm?'

'Granger never gave me your name.'

'It's Haller.' And without another word he left the cabin.

Slaughter stared at the door for a few seconds as though in a trance. Despite the guy's cold, sombre mood, he'd seemed confident. But was his confidence justified? The other three were armed and dangerous, and they wouldn't just lie down and die. Perhaps the stories Granger had told him were true. Perhaps Haller couldn't be killed. He certainly looked tough. And he'd left behind a curious smell too. A damp smell that made him think of the dog he'd owned as a boy.

Outside, the visitor walked towards the road, humming a tune to himself. Perhaps when he'd taken care of today's business and returned for his pay, he'd see if Slaughter had a few more jobs for him. Although mentally the work didn't suit him, physically, it was right up his street. He had a feeling that someone like Slaughter could keep him in work for quite some time.

4: LOCK UP

'God, I'm getting all of these! You must be thick,' Leah said, a cheeky grin on her face as she reached for her carton of juice.

'I know the answers, I just can't be bothered to shout them out.' Gerontius was beginning to get backache from leaning against the counter as he watched the contestants on *Brainbox*.

'Yeah, sure,' Leah said, listening for the next question. 'I believe you.'

'*On the periodic table, the letters Fe represent which metal?*'

'Copper! No, iron!' said Leah.

'*It's iron, Des.*'

'Yes!'

'Only the first answer counts,' Gerontius said without turning round. 'Hard luck.'

'Just because you didn't know it!' Leah shook her head.

Gerontius glanced through the window. It was different out there today. There was something strange . . . indefinable in the air.

'*OK, Debbie, well done. Now it's crunch time . . . To be this week's Brainbox, you'll need to answer the final Brainteaser. You're not nervous, are you?*'

'*Well, maybe a little, Des.*'

'*Don't worry, just relax. Now, to win the holiday for two to Florida and five thousand pounds in cash . . . tell me, Debbie . . . What animal has the Latin name* Canis Lupus?'

'The wolf!' Leah cringed when she realized what she'd done. She looked slowly across at her cousin. 'Sorry.'

'It's all right. Forget about it.' He couldn't though. Straight away the word had brought back unwelcome memories.

Just then three men entered the shop, moving past Gerontius as though he wasn't there and making for the back of the shop. They were dressed smartly, but didn't behave like businessmen. As they reached Hortense, one of them called out, 'Hey, my favourite lady!'

'Well now, who's this handsome man?' Hortense seemed pleased to see him. She laughed and gave the man a big hug.

'Hey, Mum,' the man said. 'Thought I'd drop by as I was in the area on business.'

'Ah, don't give me that rubbish – you've come for some more of my homemade coconut pie, haven't you? I know Ralphie likes it. Don't you, darling?'

'Oh yeah. Can't get enough,' the eldest of the three men said, smiling. 'I'm on a bit of a diet at the moment though, Hortense.'

'Diet? Come on, that's a dirty word around here and you know it! Ha!' They all laughed.

Gerontius tried to concentrate on the television and not look like he was eavesdropping.

The blond man, who appeared to be the youngest of the

34

three, was sniffing the air and turning his nose up. It must be the Devoida. One of the men cracked a joke and Hortense started laughing again, then said something that Gerontius couldn't quite hear. The younger man turned and walked to the front of the shop, opening a packet of crisps and stuffing a handful into his mouth. Gerontius moved away from the counter and tried to keep his eyes on the TV.

'*In a few moments, our afternoon film, but first the latest news from around the . . .*'

There was something about the men that Gerontius didn't like. The blond guy paid for the crisps and a bar of chocolate. He started checking messages on his phone, then put it down to take his change from Leah. Just then more laughter came from the back of the shop. The man turned, smiled and called out: 'I'm going to have to complain to the manager about your behaviour, Hortense.' He winked at Leah, then went back down towards his friends.

Soon afterwards they left, the two younger men laughing, the older man looking tired and bothered about something. It was only after they'd gone that Leah saw the mobile phone still lying on the counter.

'Hey, that guy left his phone.'

'What?' Gerontius, who had been leaning against the counter again, turned to face her.

'Ah, I think that's Darren's phone,' Hortense said, approaching them. 'He'd forget his head if it wasn't screwed on. Why don't you run after him, Gerry? He can't have gone far.'

Gerontius hesitated. The last thing he wanted to do was go after those men. He didn't like the look of them. But he couldn't really say no. It would have been rude.

'OK.' He picked up the phone. 'Back in a minute.' Outside the shop he looked up and down the street but couldn't see any sign of them. He wanted to go back inside and admit defeat, but he knew he should at least make an effort and see if they had turned down a side street. He broke into a jog, passing the bus stop and heading on towards the industrial estate.

When he got to the corner, he looked down the road to his right and caught sight of the three men as they turned another corner to the left. Panting already, he hurried on down the road and soon reached the left corner, looking to see how much distance he'd closed. The men were gone. He took a moment to catch his breath, then followed briskly, looking around at the old warehouses and office buildings, some in use, some abandoned, listening all the while for voices.

They were nearly at the theatre when Bale realized he'd left his phone behind.

'Hang on, guys . . .' He checked all his pockets just to make sure, but it wasn't with him. 'Damn! I left my bloody mobile at the shop. I'll go back and grab it then catch you up.'

'All right,' Mason said. 'You know where the theatre is though, right?'

'Yeah, yeah, you showed me the address. It's a couple of

streets away. I'll only be five minutes.' He turned and went back down the road at a jog.

'What is he like, eh?' Cain said, shaking his head.

Bale hadn't gone far when he heard a strange rattling whistle somewhere in the dimness of an alley to his left. He stopped and peered into the gloom, curious to identify the source of the sound. A car horn sounded in the distance, litter blew past, scuffing along the ground, but otherwise there was quiet. He was about to go on his way when he heard a voice.

'Here . . .' It came from the shadows of the alley.

Bale stepped forward cautiously. 'Who is it? Who's there?'

No reply for a few seconds, then a shuffling sound. Bale was about to reach for his gun when two lights blinked on in the darkness ahead. They were eyes . . . but the eyes of what? He was debating whether to turn and run or not when two hands sprang out of the darkness in an instant, grabbed him and pulled him in. He yelled, then groaned as something gripped him hard with one arm and started punching his head with incredible force. He couldn't move. His attacker had him in a vice-like grip, squeezing his lungs with awesome force. With the energy and breath he had left he tried to scream, and that's when the huge teeth clamped onto his neck. He choked. There was a blinding flash of colour, then everything went black.

Mason and Cain reached the theatre, though they'd nearly walked past it. Mason had expected a grand, if slightly aged façade – but instead found a sorry-looking white-brick frontage, flaking, pock-marked and defaced with layers of graffiti. If anything, it looked like a run-down cinema, the doorway crammed with rubbish and stained with all manner of unmentionable liquids.

'What a flea pit!' Cain exclaimed.

'Yeah. Can't think why Slaughter's nephew would be interested in this. Maybe it's better inside.' He took the key from his pocket as Cain raised his eyebrows in doubt.

Gerontius didn't pass the alley where Bale had been attacked. Instead he'd taken an earlier left turn which emerged onto the same road as the theatre. He saw the two men much further down, standing outside a large building. He quickened his pace, hoping to catch up with them before they disappeared from view. One of the men opened the front door and entered; the other followed. The third man must already be inside, he reasoned. Reaching the old building, he stopped a moment to catch his breath. The Emperor Theatre had certainly seen better days. Standing by a small traffic island and flanked by a pancake house and the Condor Chinese Restaurant (both closed down), it looked to Gerontius like a sad reject, a forgotten failure that had been refused the dignity of either death or rebirth, and had been left to rot. He looked around. There weren't many people about in this quiet part of Shepherd's Bush. He stared down at the phone in his hand. He didn't want to go inside, but he had a responsibility now. The phone had to be returned to its owner. He could go back to the shop and say he'd been unable to find the man, but he didn't want to be dishonest. He could also have taken it to the police station, but that seemed so silly if the man was only metres away.

The small glass panels in the front doors weren't broken, but they were filthy. Gerontius walked up to them and peered inside. Opposite him was what looked like a reception desk. The large window that had once screened it from visitors was smashed. Vandals had obviously been inside at some point. He pushed the large metal handrail he'd been resting on and the door moved inwards with barely a sound. The men hadn't locked the doors after entering. Part of him wished they had.

The foyer was dim: aside from the weak lamps on the wall it was lit only by the daylight that spilled through the entrance. In the centre, the circular reception desk stood alone – it would have been the main point of contact for visitors arriving to see a show. It was a large round cubicle, with deep red panels that were peeling away in some places. The dust everywhere was incredible. It must have been years since the building had been used. Some faded posters were still attached to the wall, while others hung by one corner, or lay pathetically on the floor. He walked round the reception desk, kicking away old sheets of newspaper and confectionery wrappers, and saw, beyond it, two sets of double doors.

He passed through the double doors and found himself in a long room that ran across behind the foyer. The carpet had once been impressive, plushy, but now it was dirty, the pattern barely visible through years of grime and black, trodden-in chewing gum. Opposite him was what had once been a bar area. The optics were all empty now, as were the cabinets below them. He walked over and leaned over the long bar itself. Broken glass littered the floor. There were old brown bottles, green ones too, some intact, some not. Gerontius recognized the names on the labels of some of the bottles. One of them was a brand his grandfather used to drink – he hadn't seen it in years. This place had been empty a long time. On either side of the long bar were doors, both of which had signs reading DRESS CIRCLE. These, Gerontius discovered, were locked.

He walked round a corner to the left and soon found himself in another bar area. A plaque on the wall read THE CAESAR BAR. Some of the original furniture remained, though the padded seats had been torn in numerous places. A couple of broken chairs lay on the floor. He stepped over one of them and passed quickly through the room and into a smaller foyer area; here he saw a pay telephone and fire escape to the left, a door opposite, and a set of double doors on the right with a sign reading STALLS. He tried these and was faced with the dark auditorium itself.

It took a while for his eyes to adjust to the dark. When they did, he was able to make out the features before him. To his left he could see the stage. Opposite him, on the other side of the vast room, were several private boxes, a couple of them quite large. Before him, long, curving rows of seats sloped down towards the stage. The carpet beneath them, like that in the bar rooms, had no doubt once been splendid, but was now only shrouded in grey. He walked down towards the small orchestra pit below the stage. From there he turned and took another good look around. At the back of the theatre was a large balcony. Even in the gloom he could see that there were seats missing, perhaps thrown over the edge by vandals long ago. The theatre couldn't have been a big success. It seemed to have been sited in an odd district, away from the main roads. He was probably far from alone in being unaware of its existence before today.

Gerontius suddenly remembered his reason for being there, and looked around for another door he could try in his search for the owner of the phone. As if in answer to his thoughts he heard a voice: '. . . going on?' It was faint, and clearly the tail end of a sentence, but it was definitely male, and it had to have come from somewhere in the building. He returned to the double doors he'd entered by and found himself back in the small foyer with the telephone. He tried the door marked STAFF ONLY, hoping that the owner of the phone was somewhere beyond.

Through the door he found an overturned sofa, an empty water cooler and the scattered pages of a magazine. He heard a sound further along the corridor and went slowly, carefully, not wanting to alert the men. He wasn't quite sure what he would say when he found them. He'd probably figure something out. In fact he was probably overreacting about the whole situation. All he was doing was returning a phone. Something as simple and as innocent as that couldn't possibly get him into trouble.

5: THEATRE OF BLOOD

Haller opened the front doors and entered the foyer, taking one last glance behind him to ensure he hadn't been seen. He was excited about what was to come. He'd rehearsed the job in his mind several times, and although he knew he'd succeed, there was still an element of doubt, of the unknown, about it. That's why he'd already despatched the youngest of them. Opportunity. When he'd seen the man break away from his friends and turn back, he knew he'd have to apprehend and kill him, or risk letting him get away.

But that kill had felt easy, too easy. He was tempted to try to make things a little more difficult for himself, but that could turn out to be foolish.

All he had to do now was secure the front doors from within, and they'd be trapped. He took out the keys that Slaughter had given him, and locked the front doors securely with both of them. Mason only had a key for one of the locks. Slaughter wasn't taking any chances.

'Let the hunt begin,' Haller said, slipping the keys back in his pocket.

He walked to the right of the reception desk and through the double doors to the main bar area. There was no one in here, but he'd pretty much expected that from the lack of noise. However, it didn't hurt to be cautious, so he moved quietly and carefully. He turned left and walked round to the Caesar Bar. Time to change again. He stopped for a moment, filling his lungs with air and holding it. He closed his eyes and tried to concentrate on evil thoughts, squeezing his nails into his palms at the same time to cause pain. Then, almost at once, the breath burst from his lungs, a prickly, itching sensation electrified his skin, and hair exploded violently all over his body.

A familiar throbbing pounded in his head; acid boiled in his stomach. It was like an anatomical apocalypse, but it never lasted too long. His bones contorted, expanded, broke and mended, all in the space of seconds. Teeth fell out, to be replaced by new, longer ones, better suited to the job of tearing and pulverizing flesh. He could feel his organs changing. It always felt like someone was reaching inside him and rummaging through his innards. His spine curved and his neck expanded with a popping sound. His nose blackened and extended out in front of him, followed by a new muzzle, coated in white and grey fur. A black-tipped tail pushed its way out of the hole he'd cut in the back of his trousers. Clenching his new paw-like fists, he flexed his muscles even as they finished re-shaping. He always wore clothes a size or two too big, so that they didn't tear. And, after much trial and error, he now had the perfect outfit to suit his second incarnation: a loose white shirt, grey cotton trousers and a long overcoat. For a creature of legend he looked pretty sharp.

This was when he usually unleashed a bellowing roar of

satisfaction. But today he restrained himself. He didn't want to give himself away to them too early. He stood still for a while, just breathing deeply in and out, allowing his new body to settle, his new senses to become attuned to the environment. The air was cold inside his bruised lungs, but the pain always got him high. He could smell the building in detail: old, musty, forgotten. He closed his muzzle and sucked more air in through his nostrils. Then he stopped. They were definitely here – he could smell them now. There was a strange chemical smell too. It was fresh, but what was it? He took a few more deep breaths and exhaled loudly, satisfied at the clouds of dust that gusted off the bar-room floor, and then headed for the doorway at the far end.

Gerontius stood on the threshold, trying to hear what was going on inside. There were only muffled, confused voices at first, disguised by the sound of rustling paper and drawers being opened and closed. Feeling more nervous than ever, he reached out and took hold of the door handle. That was when he felt, rather than heard, something approach. He was over-come by a terrible panic, and a certainty that something very bad would happen if he didn't move quickly. He turned and saw a door behind him marked STORE. In a flash he was across the corridor and inside the other room, where he quickly found a dark corner to hide in. Around him was dusty, broken furniture, useful only for giving him the cover he needed. Whatever was outside the room hadn't made a noise, but he knew it was there, and he prayed it hadn't seen him enter.

*   *   *

'This is all wrong!' Cain was shaking his head.

'Just get on with it. There's not much left. I wish Bale would hurry up.' Mason felt the same way as Cain, but he didn't want to let on. If the situation had felt odd to begin with, it now felt downright bizarre. They'd found the office Slaughter's nephew must have used, but there didn't seem to be any paperwork around worth worrying about. There were files in a small cabinet by one wall, but they were just invoices and receipts. Mason couldn't see how any of it could be considered delicate – it was all legit: deliveries of building materials, office equipment, snacks and drinks for the bars, quotes for maintenance work. And they were all over four years old. There didn't seem to be anything recent. But that wasn't the only thing that troubled him. There were two desks in the room, neither of which appeared to have been used recently, and on one of them lay a smashed computer, opened and gutted of anything useful.

'No one's been here in ages,' Cain said, scratching his head and looking uncomfortable. 'Something's up.' He hadn't wanted to take his shades off – he felt vulnerable without them – but with no decent light in the building, he'd had no choice.

'Just hold the bag,' Mason said sharply. He was kneeling before the filing cabinet and had reached deep inside to retrieve more scraps of paper. 'This is the last lot. I'll kill Bale when I get my hands on him. Where the bloody hell is he?' He stuffed the pages into the carrier bag they'd picked up at the shop.

'I hope you're going to have a word with Slaughter about this.'

'Yeah – when we get back to the yard.'

'Good. He's messing us about.' Cain punched the side of the filing cabinet. 'Son of a—'

'All right, all right. Calm down.' Mason stood up and brushed dust from his trousers.

Cain suddenly turned towards the office door. 'Did you hear something?' He waited, trying to listen.

Mason followed his gaze to the door. 'No. Come on, time to go.'

'Yeah. Sooner we're out of here, the better.' Just then Cain heard another sound – a sort of heavy breathing, or a large blast of air.

This time Mason heard it too. 'Bale? Bale, is that you?'

'Tosser,' Cain muttered, shaking his head. 'What's he playing at now?'

Haller hadn't seen Gerontius move from the door of the office to the store, but he'd picked up the smell of the Devoida again. It puzzled him, and he intended to investigate it if he had the opportunity. Right now, though, the two men on the other side of the door were his priority. It sounded like they had finished what they were doing and were ready to leave.

Just as Mason was about to reach for the door handle, something heavy hit it with a loud bang, cracking it down the middle and making it bow inwards. The two men swore and jumped backwards in surprise, before reaching inside their jackets for their guns.

There was a sound like a bull snorting, but it couldn't have been a bull. Not here. There was another thud as something hit the door again, and this time a section of wood flew off, leaving a small jagged hole. A moment's silence, then something emerged to fill the gap. What the two men saw made them open fire immediately.

'What the hell is that?' Cain screamed as he continued shooting at the door.

'I don't know,' Mason yelled above the din of the shots. He emptied his gun, then immediately reached for a fresh clip. 'But we must have got it. Cover me – I'll take a look.'

Cain kept his gun trained on the door, ready to fire if the beast reappeared. Mason stepped cautiously towards the splintered door, which was now barely hanging from its hinges.

Gerontius moved a few steps out from his hiding place, ready to dart back into the corner if he heard something he didn't like. The men had stopped firing, which must be a good sign, unless whatever he had heard snorting and growling out there had killed them. He wondered what it could have been. A wild dog? It must have been a big one judging by the noise it made. If it was still alive, it could be coming for him. Just then a man's voice interrupted his thoughts. They were alive then, and must have killed whatever was making the noise. He couldn't begin to guess what was going on, and he didn't care. He had to get out.

6: GRAND MAL

Mason held the gun out in front of him as though it was a torch, pointing his way towards the ruined door. It was quiet. He couldn't hear the unusual breathing any more, so the thing must be dead. As he leaned carefully forward into the huge hole in the door, he could already see the dimly lit corridor and the debris on the carpet. There didn't seem to be anything lurking on the other side ready to pounce, but there was no body on the floor either, just patches of blood.

'Can you see anything?' Cain called from behind him.

'Shh.' Mason motioned with his hand for the other man to stay back. He leaned forward a little more, so that his face was now sticking out through the hole.

'Mason,' Cain hissed again.

Mason turned round. 'Shut up!' From somewhere not too far away came a familiar melody.

'What's that?' Cain asked, moving up behind him. Then he heard the sound. 'Shit. It's Bale's mobile.' He reached for the door handle.

'Wait,' Mason said, looking once more through the hole in the door. 'That thing's still out there.'

'Thing? It's Bale – he's playing some sort of stupid joke.'

'What? So he could get shot at?'
'So what's his phone doing out there then?'

It hadn't occurred to Gerontius that someone might call the phone. He hadn't planned on having it in his possession for very long, so the idea hadn't crossed his mind. If it had, he'd have turned it off when he hid. It had been startlingly loud too. In the silence of the theatre it could easily have been heard by the two men or, if it was still alive, the thing that had tried to attack them. He pulled it from his pocket, crept to the door and placed it on the floor nearby. It stopped ringing and displayed the *1 missed call* message. He turned and crept back behind the junk in the back of the room, finding the darkest, most concealed spot. Just then the door opened and someone or something stepped inside.

He'd scared them – Haller had no doubt about that. It would put them on edge, cause them to panic, make mistakes. As soon as they'd started to open fire, he'd left. He didn't particularly like getting shot at, but he'd still managed to take several bullets to the back. The wounds had fizzled, closed in and sealed, squeezing the small metal slugs out of the holes in his shirt and onto the floor behind him with little tapping sounds. He would wait for the two men to pluck up enough courage to leave the room, then stalk them back to the front doors, where they would get a surprise. Once they discovered the second lock on the doors, they would have to try and force them open, giving him plenty of time to creep up behind them. Everything was going as planned, except for that awful smell. What the hell was it? He kept trying to penetrate the odour, to detect something underneath, but it was just too strong. As he crouched between two rows of seats in the auditorium, he tried to remember if he'd encountered it before. He heard a sound and cursed himself for the lapse of concentration. From where he squatted, his overcoat pooled around him, he could see practically the whole of the auditorium, and he was in a good position to hear the men making their way around the theatre. They had to move soon. They wouldn't want to hang about after the scare he'd just given them.

Mason and Cain left the office and went across to the room opposite. Just inside the door they found the phone. Cain stooped to pick it up, only a couple of metres away from Gerontius.

'Yeah, this is his all right,' he said. 'What the hell's it doing here? And where is he?'

'I don't know,' Mason said, 'but something strange is definitely going on here. Come on, let's have a good look round. Bale must be here. And keep your eyes open for that . . . thing. It could be anywhere.'

'You still sure it wasn't Bale?' Cain asked.

'Of course it wasn't him. I saw it – it was massive. And it had these sharp claws and grey hair . . .'

'What was it then?'

'I don't know,' Mason said. 'Maybe just some mad bloke in a costume – but he must have been a real hard case to take all those bullets and walk away. Anyway, what matters now is getting out of here.'

'I still think we were set up! What if Bale's part of it? He could be working for Slaughter.'

'Oh, will you listen to yourself!'

'These papers aren't important,' Cain said, shaking the bag. 'They're nothing.'

'You hang onto those,' Mason said sternly. 'If we get back to the boss without them, we won't be working for him any more.' He stared down at his feet, feeling tired all of a sudden. 'And shut up about Bale. He wouldn't stab us in the back, for Christ's sake. He's one of us.'

'Oh, come on, wise up, mate!' Cain shook his head.

'Look, something is definitely wrong here. But we don't know for sure that Slaughter is behind it, or Bale. We can't assume anything until we've got evidence.'

'I've got all the evidence I need,' Cain said.

'No, what you've got is a hunch, and nothing to back it up with. If we go back to the boss making wild accusations—'

'All right. Well, let's just split first, ask questions later.'

They exited the room, leaving Gerontius able to breathe properly again. He'd been terrified that he'd make a noise and draw gunfire. But they had the phone back now: the job was done. All he had to do was get out. He just prayed that nothing would try and stop him.

'The auditorium is that way,' Mason said, pointing to the double doors. They were in the small foyer with the telephone now. 'Do we go through there or round through the bars?'

'Can we get to the front doors through there?'

'I presume so. There should be several exits in there. Might even be emergency exits we can use. I just have a bad feeling about the other way.'

'It'll be quicker going through the bar,' Cain insisted.

'Yeah, but that might be what it's hoping we'll think. Hang on.' Mason took out his mobile phone. 'I'm going to call Slaughter. See what he says about all this.' He took the mobile from Cain and started punching in Slaughter's office number.

Cain shook his head. 'I bet you he doesn't answer. I wouldn't . . .'

Sure enough, it continued to ring until Mason lost patience and cancelled the call. 'Shit! Maybe he's just out of the cabin.'

'Huh, yeah, he's out of his cabin all right. He's made a big mistake.'

'We're wasting time. Let's go.' Mason opened the double doors and stepped cautiously into the auditorium; Cain, also with gun drawn, followed close behind.

Mason could see two green emergency exit signs on either side of the stage. He pointed towards them and Cain nodded in understanding. They moved down the left side of the theatre, careful not to lose their footing on the steps in the gloom, and stopped when they both saw two small yellow lights, unblinking in the darkness of a row of seats to their right.

'Oh shit,' Cain said, the fear almost paralysing him. 'Shit, Mason, I can't move my arm.'

'Can you move your legs?'

'What?'

'Run!' It had only been a whisper, but in the silence of the vast theatre it seemed louder. They turned and hurtled back up the steps towards the double doors. As Cain flung them open and went through, Mason tripped and fell flat. The air was pushed from his lungs as he landed on his stomach. Cursing, he quickly got back on his feet and left the auditorium, not daring to look behind.

Once the second man had left, Haller took a good sniff of the air. He could smell their fear. It was pungent. He sniffed again, then moved along the row of seats until he reached the steps. He'd been crouched for some time, so he stood up straight and stretched a little. It wouldn't be long now. They were panicking, scared. The work would be over in minutes. He made fists with his paws, the claws prodding the thick pads of his palms again to keep him focused. He sighed as he walked up the steps, speculating on how the men would die.

Mason was about to turn left and run for the foyer when he heard a noise to his right. Glancing back in that direction, he saw the door opposite the office swinging slowly back into place. What the hell was Cain playing at? It was stupid to go and hide in that room when their priority was to get out of the building.

'Shit!' He ran over to the store, his hand on his gun, ready to draw it if the beast was following him. Opening the door, he was surprised to find nothing but the same junk that had been there before.

'Cain?' Nothing. 'Cain, for God's sake, are you in here?' Still no sound, until something near the far wall fell to the floor. 'Cain? What the bloody hell are you doing?' He picked his way through the piled-up furniture, becoming more and more angry and confused by the second. And he was surprised to say the least when he saw the terrified boy crouched in the corner.

Haller reached the top of the steps and passed through the double doors, then through the Caesar Bar until he emerged in the large bar area behind the foyer. The black man's scent was strong now, but the other man's was much less so. They would surely stay together though: splitting up was pointless if they both wanted to get out of the building. Then he heard a panicked voice – a harsh whisper. The man clearly wanted to shout but kept it down, perhaps for fear of being heard.

'Mason, where are you? We've got to get out of here!'

Cain was sure they'd left the front door open, but it wouldn't budge. It was locked. Mason had the key, but Cain couldn't wait for him to catch up. He looked around for a container or recess in the foyer that might be hiding something he could use to force the door open, but there was nothing. *Damn it!* He went back to the doors and tried pulling them again. No luck. They might be old but they were still sturdy. He was about to draw his gun and try shooting the lock off when he heard the creak of a door opening behind him. Someone was approaching, and they were trying not to make any noise.

Although the foyer carpet was soft, it couldn't mask the sound of footsteps completely, especially with the many items of detritus scattered about. There was suddenly a smell of stale breath. Cain gasped involuntarily and shivered. He didn't want to turn round, but there was little choice.

'Mason – is that you?'

'Yeah,' came the reply, but it was a voice he didn't recognize. A deep, guttural sound, barely human at all.

With a great effort Cain made himself turn and face the source of the sound. His eyes widened in shock. It definitely wasn't Mason. It wasn't Bale either. The clothes it wore were unfamiliar. It stood no more than two metres away, a huge, dark shape with burning eyes. Its tongue lolled from a large, dog-like muzzle that oozed saliva in steady strands. *My God.* Cain began to question his sanity. The creature wore a long raincoat over a white shirt. It licked its lips as it stood there just watching him. *Where are you, Mason?* he pleaded silently.

///

7: No Way Out

It was a miracle Gerontius was still alive. Mason's finger had been on the trigger, ready to squeeze it. He hadn't expected anyone else to be in the building. He lowered the gun and looked down at the boy, who was trying in vain to mouth some sort of a response.

'Who the hell are you?' Mason demanded. 'Were you the one at the door?' Even as he spoke the words he knew the answer was no. The kid couldn't have made that much noise, or caused that much damage. And besides, he looked terrified. Mason's anger subsided. He felt sorry for the youngster. He'd probably never had a gun pointed at him before. Their eyes remained locked for a few moments until Mason returned the gun to the shoulder holster inside his jacket and beckoned the boy out from behind the jumble of furniture.

Gerontius didn't know what to do. It was hard to trust someone who had pointed a gun at him.

'What the hell are you doing here? You nearly got killed.' There was genuine concern in Mason's voice.

'I . . . I just came to give the phone back. Honestly.'

'Phone? So that was you. Wait . . . You were at the Express Mart, weren't you?'

'Yeah. Your friend left his phone on the counter. Hortense

asked me to run after him. I didn't really want to but—'

'Do you know where Bale is? The one who left his phone behind?' Mason looked towards the door. 'Did you see where he went?'

'No. I haven't seen him since the shop.'

'All right, well, come on. My friend should be waiting for me in the foyer. There's something very dangerous here – some kind of animal.'

'Are you sure it's an animal?'

'Well, it didn't sound like a man, but . . . What's your name anyway?'

'Gerontius.'

'No kidding.'

'It's from *The Dream of Gerontius*—'

'By Elgar . . . yeah.'

'You know it?'

'I like classical music,' Mason replied. 'My name's Mason, but you can—'

Mason's words were interrupted by a bloodcurdling scream from the direction of the foyer. His mouth dropped open and his hand reached for his gun.

They passed quickly through the two bar areas, Mason feeling guilty that he had delayed in following Cain. The scream had unnerved him. Men like Cain weren't supposed to scream. He called over his shoulder: 'You all right?'

'Yeah, I'm OK,' Gerontius said, but he was terrified.

Mason sensed this, and wasn't surprised. But considering the circumstances, the boy could be taking it a lot worse.

*   *   *

Cain couldn't help but scream. Every childhood nightmare seemed to be converging on him at that point. The creature stood up straight now, revealing its full height and towering over him. It had to be well over two metres tall. Cain could see its tongue moving from side to side as it sniffed the air. What was somehow clear to Cain then was that the creature wasn't just going to kill him – it was going to tear him to pieces.

It took another step closer. Cain managed to put a hand on his gun and draw it slowly out of the holster, trying not to provoke a reaction. He doubted whether the gun would do him any good. He and Mason had fired a shower of bullets at the creature earlier, without any noticeable effect. The thing took yet another step towards him, and caught the light from the door. *Oh . . . Jesus, no*, Cain thought as the monster was fully revealed.

Cain had read about werewolves and had seen them depicted on television and in movies. He didn't believe in them though. They were complete fantasy . . . Yet this thing could be nothing else. Its body was essentially humanoid, except for the legs, which were longer and had an extra segment in the foot so that the thing seemed to be standing on tiptoe with its knees bent. It was wearing shoes, but its hairy, padded claws stuck out of holes cut in the front. And the head . . . The head was like a wolf's, but bigger, and with the gleam of human intelligence in its eyes. It licked its jaws again.

'What do you want?' Cain asked. Without him realizing it, his hand had fallen away from the gun, and he had pressed himself against the door behind him. The creature issued a low, prolonged growl in reply, then sucked in a huge breath before blowing it out in one loud, long blast. The resulting smell that assaulted Cain was awful. He coughed, trying to rid his airways of the foul stink. The jaws opened, and in the resulting split second while the creature's eyes were closed, Cain ducked out of the way and back across the foyer to the double doors, which he flung open, before running straight into Mason.

Mason lowered his gun. He looked startled.

'Jesus, you gave me a—'

'Come on,' Cain hissed, registering the boy but knowing it was the wrong time for questions. 'It's right behind me.' He ran off, Cain and Gerontius following close behind. They rushed down the bar to the right, turned left past the ladies' toilets and then stopped halfway along the corridor by a door marked STUDIO. Cain ushered Mason and the boy into the room and, taking one last look outside, followed, closing the door behind him.

Back in the foyer, Haller padded across the carpet, taking his time, knowing the man couldn't escape while his scent was still so strong in his airways. Perhaps the pursuit would add some excitement to the proceedings. By the time he reached the bar area beyond the foyer doors, the black man had disappeared. He could still smell him though, as well as the other man – and that smell that reminded him of disinfectant. He took a few confirming sniffs, his black nose wrinkling as he did so, then moved down the room to the right, following the man's scent. He stopped at the door to the ladies' toilets and listened. He could hear dripping and there was a plane passing somewhere far overhead. He gripped the door handle and twisted.

Inside the toilets, Haller stopped for a moment to look at himself in the cracked mirror. After all this time he still found the sight awe-inspiring. He would never have believed such a thing possible if he hadn't experienced it first hand. He moved closer, steaming the mirror's surface with the breath from his nostrils. He loved the eyes, so beautifully golden-yellow, and the teeth, the interlocking upper and lower canines, long and sharp, designed to mince flesh in seconds. He thought briefly of that fateful moment when his life had taken such a drastic turn. The creature that had attacked him had taken great pleasure in its victim's fear. Haller could almost appreciate that now, could almost sympathize. He made a 'hmph' sound, then turned to leave the room. There was no time for self-indulgence. Not now. He had a job to do.

8: UNFINISHED BUSINESS

'Jesus Christ, that thing!' Cain leaned his ear against the door, listening for any sound that might indicate the beast's approach. He turned briefly to look at the other two. 'Who are you?' Cain eyed Gerontius suspiciously.

'His name's Geron— er, Gerry,' Mason said.

'What the hell's he doing here?'

'He came here to return Bale's phone,' Mason said, looking around the room.

'Return it?'

'Yeah, he left it at the shop. Look, what the hell is out there?'

'You'd have to see it to believe it.'

'What do you mean?'

'Maybe . . . maybe it got Bale on the way here – and that's why he hasn't turned up.'

There was a pause as the two men tried to get their heads around the situation.

'What are we going to do?' Gerontius looked from man to man, hoping one of them had a suggestion.

'We must have a few bullets left between us,' Mason said. 'We have to find the nearest exit, and if necessary blast our way out.'

'And if that thing finds us? Bullets don't seem to do any good.'

'I don't know – maybe it'll just go.' But Mason doubted this.

'No way. It came here to kill us . . . I reckon Slaughter sent it.'

'Look, don't start that again. If it's just some wild animal or—'

'It's not an animal! It's a bloody—'

'What?' Mason went to the door and put his ear against it.

'I saw it up close. I'm telling you, you wouldn't believe me if—'

'Try me.'

Haller picked up the scent trail again as he left the toilets and considered his options. He didn't want to confront both men together if he could help it. It would be an exciting challenge, but a little too risky. It would be better to take them on individually. He walked round the corner and approached the door to the studio, which was to the side of the auditorium. He sniffed round the door. They were in there, cowering, no doubt, feeding each other's anxiety. Good. Panic led to poor judgement, hasty decisions. The small corridor ended a short way in front of him. He found another set of doors to the auditorium and entered quietly, creeping towards the back wall, where he could listen to the activity in the studio without being discovered.

* * *

'So what is it then?'

'Well, I guess it is some sort of animal,' Cain lied, feeling the boy's eyes on him, not wanting to scare him with the truth. 'It wasn't a bloke in a costume or anything, it was real. It had these bright eyes . . . and a tongue, and drool and everything. Jesus, I've never been so scared in my life. I thought it was going to eat me.'

'Just now you said it wasn't an animal,' Mason said, confused. He paced around.

'Yeah, well, I wasn't thinking straight.'

'Well, we're going nowhere until we've dealt with it, whatever it is. So I think we need to go on the offensive.'

'What?'

'The boy can hide in here while we go and find it.'

'No way!' Gerontius yelled, unable to help himself. 'You can't leave me alone.'

'Look, you'll be OK as long as you don't make any noise. We won't be long, I promise.'

'Mason,' Cain said in a whisper, not wanting the boy to hear. 'I don't think we can do anything to this thing. It's huge, and it didn't seem to mind being shot to pieces earlier.'

'Well, it was lucky that time.'

As the men debated, Gerontius prayed that the animal, whatever it was, would just go and leave them alone. Dark, unwanted memories were resurfacing again, and he was trying as hard as he could to block them, deny them.

Cain looked at Gerontius with a degree of uncertainty. 'You sure he'll be safe in here?'

'That thing's only interested in us. It won't waste its time with him while we're wandering around looking for it.'

'I hope you're right.'

'Listen, Gerry,' Mason said, walking over to the boy. 'When we leave, I want you to pile as much of this furniture against the door as you can, OK? And don't move it until we come back for you.'

'What if you don't come back?'

'We will. All right?' Mason seemed certain.

Gerontius nodded in reply. He didn't like the idea of barricading himself into a room without knowing what was going on, but he had to trust them. The two men checked their guns, then moved to the door. Cain opened it a little and peered outside.

'It's clear.'

'OK, let's go.' As he was about to leave, Mason turned to Gerontius and said: 'We will be back – trust me.' And then he was gone.

Gerontius felt a sudden chill and panic now that he was on his own. How could they leave him? But there was no time for that now. He tried to concentrate on what he had to do. He grabbed two old padded chairs and pushed them on their casters to the door. He tried to jam the back of one of them under the door handle, but it wouldn't fit. He looked around and saw what he guessed was a large speaker. Walking over to it, he saw that this too was on wheels so he rolled it over as well. It was heavy, but he doubted it would stop someone forcing his way in. Nothing else in the room looked like it would do the trick. He would have to find something else, something bigger and heavier. He moved the makeshift barricade aside, then opened the door a fraction and peered into the corridor outside. There had to be something close by that he could use.

Haller's confusion was growing. Although he'd been certain there were just two men in the studio, he was sure he'd heard a youth. But that didn't make any sense. He hadn't smelled anyone else. And no one else was meant to be here. He was curious, and a little concerned. If someone else was here, he had to know. He could make out the men's voices again. They were approaching the auditorium doors. Maybe they had guessed that he would return here after nearly cornering one of them in the foyer. He had to avoid them long enough to get to the studio and see if there was a third person. If there was, he would have to deal with him. Just then he again detected the smell of disinfectant, and another smell beneath it, possibly human. His nose twitched in frustration. He had to find the source of that smell.

Mason looked at the luminous dials on his watch and saw that it was now nearly four o'clock. He and Cain were both standing by the auditorium doors, unsure what exactly to do next.

'Cain?'

'Yeah?'

'How close did this thing get to you?'

'Pretty close.'

There was an uneasy pause.

'So?'

'So what?'

'So what the hell is it? You must know.'

'I didn't want to say anything in front of the kid.' Cain sighed, not really wanting to explain what had happened and what he had seen. 'I didn't want to scare him.'

'Whatever it is, it can pull a door apart with its hands and take bullets like they were kisses! Now what is it?'

'I . . . I'm still not sure I want to believe what I saw, but . . . I think it was a werewolf.'

'What?' Mason shook his head, then massaged his temples. 'This doesn't make any sense. All right, look, it doesn't matter what it is – let's just kill it and get the hell out of here. Before it kills us.'

'Right.'

'Right.' Mason slowly pushed open the door in front of him and entered the auditorium, his gun held out, waiting for the slightest movement.

They made their way down the steps carefully. Once they reached the stage, they climbed onto it and found the long workshop behind it. At the far end was a small boiler room, inside which was a boarded-up exit door that they might be able to break open. The fluorescent lighting was poor, and both men were aware that the monster could be lurking anywhere in the many shadows. Without exchanging a word, they began checking the whole of the workshop, ready to unload their weapons at the slightest provocation. When they were satisfied that they were alone, they returned to the boiler room and walked past the long-silenced machines and pipes to stand before the fire exit. It was not only locked and boarded, but had also been secured with a heavy chain and padlock.

'All right,' Cain said. 'Let's blast this to pieces and get the hell out of here!'

'Wait – what about that thing? We can't just forget about it.'

'*I* can! I'm getting out of here.'

'Look, if we don't do something now it could carry on following us. I don't want to have to keep looking over my shoulder for it. Besides, we can't leave Gerry here.'

'Forget him! It's his fault he—'

'Don't you dare! There's no way we're leaving him alone with that thing. He doesn't deserve any of this.'

'Oh, and *we* do?' They were both silent for a few moments. 'Fine then,' Cain said, making a decision. 'You want to stay? Stay. I'm going.'

Gerontius was about to creep out of the room in search of more furniture for the barricade when he saw it. A black, twitching nose at first, then the muzzle, jaws, eyes, ears – the whole head – and a huge, hunched body clad in men's clothing. He couldn't believe it. This was the creature that had attacked the men in the office? This nightmare vision that had found him again? Not content with bringing pain and death into his life once, it was here again. There could only be one explanation, he realized as he darted behind one of the old lighting consoles. The monster had returned to finish what it had started eight years ago.

He shook, a new chill of terror racking his body. He could almost see his breath pluming from his mouth as the temperature in the studio seemed to drop. His vision blurred, and he imagined he could see snowflakes seesawing gently towards the floor. And a sound of hissing somewhere close by . . .

|||

9: THE PARALYSING CLAW

Eight years ago

The hissing, he guessed, must be the engine – or the radiator, he wasn't sure which. Some time after the car had stopped rolling, he had blacked out. Now, weird sounds and smells came to him. He was dimly aware of something terrible taking place nearby, though exactly what he didn't know. He hadn't the energy to force himself properly awake. Time passed as he swam into and out of a semi-lucidity, until at last he opened his eyes and was welcomed to a scene of madness.

His shoulders ached. His wrists ached. His neck had been hurt too. In fact it felt like his whole skeleton had been stretched in every direction, then snapped back into place like elastic. For a moment he had no idea where he was, or what he was doing there. Then, slowly, he remembered Austria, the holiday . . . But what was wrong with the car? His body wasn't sitting but hanging from the seat. The car must be upside down. He could hear music – the radio. He recognized the song but it didn't feel right. It was distorted, twisted into a sinister version of itself.

Looking around, he saw that it was early evening, with

darkness already descending. He couldn't see either of his parents in front of him, and moving his position slightly, he was able to confirm with some alarm that both of the front seats were vacant and the front passenger door seemed to be missing. Where were they? And why had they left him all alone? The dashboard was a mess from the deployment of the airbags. They'd been wearing their seat belts, so they couldn't have been thrown out. But he couldn't see anything more from his position. He would have to get out of the car.

He groaned and tried to move. Something slipped and he dropped further, banging his head on the roof of the car. He groaned and waited for the nausea to subside. Moving his legs, he tried to put his feet on the roof while he fumbled for the seat-belt release. It was hard to reach, and the effort hurt his already sore arms. He clicked the catch open and his body slumped down onto the car's roof, which was now the floor. He crouched there like a trapped animal, growing more and more uneasy with this new upside-down world he'd awoken to. Another wave of dizziness washed over him, and he had to wait for his head to clear before he could move again.

It was getting darker all the while, and colder too. The radio was still belting out music. He slowly gripped and pulled the door catch to his left. Pushing outward, he found that the door didn't want to move. He put all his strength into it and managed to move it a couple of centimetres. As if his throbbing head and aching body weren't bad enough, his stomach now started turning. The door wasn't going to move by persuasion alone; it needed brute force. He drew his knees up almost to his face, then kicked out hard in front of him with both feet. Metal screamed in protest, but the gap widened. He repeated the process, and this time the door, which he could now see had been damaged by the crash, swung open with a groan, hanging by one warped hinge. He shuffled forward and climbed through the gap into the cold snow outside.

Initially, the car didn't look as bad as he'd expected. Walking a few paces to his left, he could see that the bonnet had sheered to one side. Steam hissed in a thick, angry plume, melting the snow beneath before twisting towards the sky. He looked all around for the car's missing occupants, but could see nothing. Behind him the ground sloped away down the hillside and into the valley below. Far off, at the eastern end of the valley, there was still some light, evidence of the final, clinging grasp of the sun. There was no sign of his parents in the immediate area. But if they'd been conscious, they would never have left him alone in the car. Surely one of them would have stayed with him while the other went for help? He crouched by the vehicle and looked through the window of the driver's door. Wiping the snow away from the glass, he could see what he hadn't been able to before: not only had the front passenger door been removed, but both seat belts were shredded. Not torn, not snapped . . . shredded. He stood up straight and looked over the underside of the car to the slope that led back up to the road. There was a dark object some metres beyond the vehicle. It could be the missing door. But it was quite a distance away. It must have come loose in the roll. Unless someone had been thrown . . .

He walked very slowly round the front of the car, hoping at any moment to hear the call of his mother or father, followed by a hug and a reassurance that everything was fine. He felt cold, not just because of the temperature, but because he was already in shock, already feeling the effects of the horror that had yet to be fully unveiled. Reaching the front passenger opening, he saw deep, ragged claw marks in the door frame. Terror hit him like a punch as he remembered the thing that had landed on the bonnet and caused his father to lose control of the car and roll over the edge of the road. *Oh my God*, he thought. *Where is it now? What has it done with Mum and Dad?* He whirled round, searching the whole area with his eyes, ready to react to the merest hint of movement. It could be nearby. It could be watching him right now.

The darkness of the trees might be concealing so much. Looking back up the slope towards the road, all he could see was a series of trenches in the snow, made by the car in its clumsy descent. There was nothing but shadow everywhere else. It was hard to make anything of the gloom around him. He looked back inside the car and now saw claw marks on the seat and the dashboard. There was a dark liquid pooled in a small corner of the roof near the jagged edge of the ruined windscreen. It had already started to congeal. There were also dots and spatters on the rear-view mirror and the CD player. He started swaying, wondering if he was going to lose consciousness again. The driver's side door hadn't been opened. And there had been no need. The monster had dragged both his parents out of the passenger side, possibly after it had wrenched the door from the frame and tossed it away. He reached forward and silenced the radio. Now all he could hear was the wind . . . and something else.

It was the wet, tearing sound of meat being wrenched from the bone. His stomach convulsed. Turning to his left, he could now see, through the trees, another small open patch of snow. In it something was hunched over a pile of clothes, its face buried. The head twitched a few times as the beast swallowed its meal. It looked up and stopped a moment, turning to fix him with its two burning eyes. There was a moment of terror, when it seemed certain that the creature would bound towards him and tear him apart. But it didn't; it merely dipped its head and resumed feeding, as though Gerontius was of no immediate concern. *Oh God*, he thought, realizing what the pile of clothes was. *That's my mum it's eating . . . That's my mum!* He could only stand and stare in shock as the thing continued to devour his mother, knowing that he could do nothing, that it was far too late. As he tilted his head upwards, it seemed the clouds were swirling around him, but they weren't. He was fainting.

The emergency services arrived over an hour later. Somehow he had found his way back inside the car, though he had no memory of doing so. A passing motorist must have discovered the wreck and alerted the authorities. A woman in uniform told the shivering boy that he was lucky not to have caught pneumonia. He could see that the situation had troubled her. Had she been near the bodies and seen what had been done to them? He tried to identify the spot where his parents' bodies lay, but the people around him kept blocking his view, telling him that everything was going to be all right. Blinking through the warm tears, he called out for them over and over again, without reply. Shock continued to grip him in its icy, paralysing claw, as it would do for many days . . .

Trees faded from the periphery of his vision, snowflakes disappeared, the temperature returned to normal and he was back in the dusty studio. Had the creature really been searching for him for the last eight years? If so, what had taken it so long, and why was he so important to it? The sickening feeling in the pit of his stomach deepened.

After some minutes had passed, Gerontius actually thought the creature might have gone away. He hadn't heard any sounds for a while. But then, with a horror-movie inevitability, there came the sound of breathing from outside the room, and claws scraping along wood. He hadn't tried to barricade the door after running back in, and it wasn't locked. The thing could be inside in seconds. This was it. This was the sound of death. The door handle began to turn, there was another snort of breath, then— A gunshot, followed by someone yelling, then more gunshots. The creature growled, and then, incredibly, it left. Realizing he had been holding his breath, Gerontius exhaled.

* . * . *

'Just wait.' Before Mason had a chance to continue, Cain fired another shot at the door, blasting chunks and splinters all over the room.

'Will you fucking listen?' Mason grabbed Cain's hand and wrestled for the gun.

'Get off me!'

'Well calm down then.'

'Calm down?' Cain fired several more shots into the wood, opening up a large chunk near the lock. He grabbed the bar across the door and pulled. Nothing. 'Shit!'

'Stop that! It'll hear you!'

'If you gave me a hand, we'd be out of here before it finds us.'

'I told you! We're not leaving the kid.'

'What's the matter with you?' Cain turned from the door, ejected the empty clip from his gun and fitted a full one.

'For Christ's sake, Cain – I think we can kill that thing.'

'Look, if that thing's invincible and we waste these bullets trying to kill it, we're screwed. We need to use them to break apart this door so we can get out. Once we're back in the outside world you'll forget about that thing and that kid. Trust me.'

'Trust you?' Mason gave his partner a distasteful look.

Cain looked at his feet, then at his gun. 'Look . . . I don't want the kid to die. Seriously. But if we don't look after ourselves, we could all end up dead – or worse. Do you want to turn into one of those things? I know I bloody don't.'

'What do you mean?'

'You've seen the films – if you get bitten by a werewolf, you turn into one.'

'You don't know that for sure.'

'Yeah, well, I'm not waiting around to find out.'

'All right . . . Just give me five minutes, OK? I'll go fetch Gerry, then we'll get out of here.'

'And what if you meet that thing on the way?'

'I'll deal with that if it happens. Wait here . . . All right?'

'You've got five minutes.'

'Right.' Mason turned and jogged back down the length of the workshop, through the open door back into the corridor that ran along past the office they'd ransacked earlier. As he passed the doors to the auditorium, he had no idea that Haller was only metres away on the other side, making his way down the steps to the stage, and the workshop door beyond.

Cain swore his impatience, and as the slow seconds ticked by, he grew more and more uncomfortable. Remaining in the boiler room, not taking any decisive action, was agony. His attention stayed fixed on the door. He had to mentally force himself to leave it alone until Mason returned. It was perhaps the hardest thing he'd ever done. Escape lay on the other side, and the temptation to reach out and grab it was overwhelming. Three minutes had passed since Mason had left him. Would he be justified in taking off alone if Mason hadn't returned after the five minutes were up? Maybe. Maybe not. Something moved in the workshop. It sounded like the whine of a door hinge. Perhaps Mason was back already. Cain went to the door of the boiler room and opened it a little. He was in time to see one of the three long fluorescent tubes on the ceiling smash, leaving a large section of shadow on the other side of the room and a sprinkling of broken glass on the floor. His brow furrowed in confusion. Something flew through the air and hit the second tube. There were sparks, then more shadow. He moved his head to try and see what was going on, and in the instant before the third projectile flew towards its target, plunging the workshop into complete darkness, he saw the beast crouched by a door to his left.

As it panted, its shoulders rose and fell. Cain could tell this from the way the burning yellow eyes bobbed up and down rhythmically. He tried not to make a sound. There was no definite sign that it had seen him yet, but it must know that someone was in here, otherwise it wouldn't have bothered with the lights. He saw the eyes move. The creature was backing away from him, down the length of the room, sniffing all the while. *Mason? Where the hell are you?* he screamed silently. He knew he would be trapped if he stayed in the boiler room. He had to reach the door to the stage, and then maybe he could find Mason. He opened the boiler-room door wider, praying it wouldn't make any noise. When there was a big enough gap, he squeezed through into the workshop, keeping his eyes fixed on the darkness ahead, ready for any sign of those eyes, and holding onto his gun for dear life.

10: EXIT STAGE LEFT

Gerontius didn't want to move. He didn't want to leave the room. But the monster had been so close. It must have known he was in there, so it could be back at any moment. The longer he waited, the more time the creature had to kill the two men and come back for him. He stood up and walked over to the door. After listening for a while, he opened it slowly and looked out into the corridor.

Apart from the fact that there was no approaching monster, the view was the same as he remembered. He had to get as far away from this nightmare as possible before it was too late.

He left the room quietly and closed the door behind him. Creeping with the utmost stealth, he reached the main bar area and listened. Nothing. Then he was aware of something approaching to his right. He knew he was going to scream as he turned to face it, but the sound never emerged. It was Mason, holding out one hand to placate him – or to keep him quiet, it wasn't clear which.

'It's OK,' he told him. 'We found an exit in the workshop. Should have it open without too much trouble. We have to go now – I've no idea where that thing is.'

'It was here a few minutes ago,' Gerontius said as they hurried off.

'Well, maybe it lost interest. Come on—'

There was a strange, muffled sound, like breaking glass. They stopped at the entrance to the Caesar Bar.

'What was that?' Gerontius asked.

'I don't know.' They heard the sound again, then once more. 'Come on, we're wasting time.'

Haller knew exactly where the black man was. But it was safer to lure him out of his hiding place, to catch him off guard. After he'd dealt with the lights, he moved down towards the end of the workshop opposite the boiler room and waited.

Cain was shaking. He carefully rose up so that he could see over the surface of the table he was crouching behind. There was nothing coming. He ducked down again. To his left, only metres away, was the door to the stage. If he moved fast enough he could reach it before the creature caught him, but if he made the slightest noise, it would immediately be in hot pursuit. He had to do it quietly, stealthily, putting some distance between himself and the workshop before his absence was noticed.

Haller stopped moving and inhaled. Just from his scent, he could tell where the man was. He looked around at the shelving that was bolted to the walls on either side, running the whole length of the room. There was just enough space along the top for him to move without making a sound. He walked over to the opposite stack of shelves and climbed them effortlessly. He then moved carefully along on all fours until he was opposite the spot where the man was choosing his moment to escape. Haller tensed his muscles, ready to spring.

Cain couldn't hear the creature, much less see it. *It could have left the workshop at the far end*, he thought, though he knew this was likely to be wishful thinking. His eyes scoured the dark all around him for any sign of movement, and then he saw it. It wasn't its eyes he spotted first this time, but the sharp outline of its ears, grey against the blackness around it. There it was, sitting atop the shelving, appearing to grin down at him, its hands ready to propel itself forwards. He raised the gun, but he was too slow. The beast flew towards him and landed on his chest as the bullet went wild.

Cain yelled as they both crashed to the floor, the creature on top of him, scattering rubbish. He acted quickly, pushing the beast with his feet, so that it toppled backwards, stumbling into the shelves behind. He'd held onto the gun, which he now pointed towards it. It grunted its annoyance as it tried to get back onto its feet. Cain fired once. The creature fell backwards, shook its head, then got up again. He fired a second time, and a third, and a fourth. It stayed down, but it was still making noises. He emptied the magazine into it and it fell silent. Werewolf or not, there was nothing on earth that could survive that.

Cain turned and was about to run to the door when he heard a sound behind him. Wheeling round, he saw the creature stand and bare its teeth at him, saliva and blood dripping from its jaws, anger burning in its eyes. Despite the shaking of his body – either from the adrenaline or the fear – he managed to reload his gun and raised it once more. He fired twice, then dived over one of the centre tables onto the floor on the other side, rolling as far away as he could before once more aiming his weapon at the beast. It was on the table and heading in his direction. He rolled behind a heavy crate, feeling his heart pounding in his ribcage.

'Why not make it easy on yourself?' the creature said. It spoke in a deep, rasping growl that sounded forced and awkward. The sound was anything but human. 'You're going to die anyway.'

Cain went cold as the thought of imminent death now consumed him. 'What do you want?' He could sense its proximity now. It was only a couple of metres away. It had stopped moving and Cain could smell its horrible breath again.

In what could have been his final seconds, Cain pushed himself away from the crate and fired at the beast, which had been about to grab him. One of the bullets went straight through the creature's left eye. It howled in pain and raised one paw to its ruined eye socket. Cain fired more shots until he'd emptied the gun, then ran straight to the stage door, opening it with one swift movement and plunging into the area beyond.

Although the lighting in the auditorium was minimal, it was still preferable to the awful darkness of the workshop. Cain darted across the stage, nearly slipping on the smooth surface, then dropped down into the orchestra pit. He heard a bellow of pain and rage behind him, and turned to see the creature lunging across the stage, gore pouring from its eye socket. As Cain stood frozen in terror, it howled again, and jumped through the air and down into the pit, pinning him to the ground and pushing the breath from his lungs with all the force of a sledgehammer.

Mason reached the end of the corridor and burst into the workshop, realizing it could already be too late for Cain. Gerontius followed closely, prepared to turn and flee at the first hint of trouble. The room was in darkness, and they couldn't hear anything except— A cry, from somewhere in the auditorium. Mason led the way down the room and found the stage door on the right.

'Stay here – hide if you have to, but don't move until I come back.' He gripped the door handle, and as he turned it, Gerontius ducked and crawled under the nearest table. He felt helpless. He didn't want the men to die, but what could he do?

Cain had no more bullets, and he knew that without them he was as good as dead. The monster stepped off him and allowed him to get to his feet. Cain began backing away towards the steps, holding his hands out as if they could ward off the creature.

'Please, please, don't do it. I can pay you.'

The monster slowly shook its head from side to side, giving the man a clear message. Then it opened its jaws, glaring at him with its one burning eye. In a second it had closed the distance between them and grabbed Cain's shoulders, the claws biting through his clothes and into his flesh.

'It wasn't our fault, I promise you! It wasn't—'

The claws sank deeper and Cain screamed, the sound turning to a gargle as large teeth clamped forcefully onto his neck.

From the stage, Mason witnessed the whole scene, heard the awful sound as the creature bit into his friend's flesh. His stomach turned and he thought he was going to be sick. He wanted to shout something, but it was too late now. Cain was being shaken like a rag doll. His remaining energy ebbed with each attempt to free himself from those powerful teeth. Worst of all, his bulging eyes were fixed in Mason's direction. He seemed to be silently pleading for help. But what could Mason do? If he tried to kill the thing now and failed, none of them would get out alive. He had a responsibility, and unfortunately it meant leaving Cain to die. But although he knew he should run back to the boiler room and get out of there with the boy while there was still time, he was rooted to the spot. Then, incredibly, Cain's lips moved and mouthed the word 'Go'. And, in a final act of defiance, the savaged man screamed, tore his attacker's jaws from his neck and forced the beast to the ground, holding onto it as hard as he could, even as it raked his body with its claws. Cain's new-found strength wouldn't last long. But perhaps it would buy Mason enough time. *Thanks, Cain*, Mason thought as he ran back into the workshop.

'Stand back against that wall and cover your face. There'll be a fair amount of shrapnel.' Mason had wasted no time in getting himself and the boy into the boiler room. They had minutes, perhaps even seconds left to make their escape. Gerontius stood against the wall opposite the emergency exit, then squatted down, folding his arms around his knees. As Mason stood back and aimed at the wood, Gerontius leaned forward, burying his head.

The sound was deafening. Bits of wood flew all over the place, many landing on his neck, his arms and even down the back of his sweatshirt. He heard Mason swear more than once, no doubt because he'd been injured by the pieces of flying debris. When Mason had used up all his bullets, he pulled off the clip and let it fall to the floor while he reached for another.

Mason knew there was nothing he could have done for Cain. The risk had been far too great, especially with the boy's safety to consider. And Cain could well have bought them the time they needed to escape. He looked at Gerontius. The boy was covered in bits of wood. *Poor kid, he's too young for this shit*, he thought. The shots rang out once more, as round after round thudded into the door. Suddenly, one of the links in the thick chain shattered, and the padlock fell to the floor. Mason fired again. The second shot blew a large splinter of wood from the doorframe straight into his side. He screamed, then immediately tried to stifle the sound.

Gerontius looked up. 'What happened?'

'Nothing – just a splinter, that's all. Nearly there.' Mason gingerly gripped the end of the sliver and drew it out, gritting his teeth against the pain as he did so. He dropped it on the floor and noticed the blood already staining his shirt. Ignoring his wound for the moment, he continued firing.

When the second magazine had emptied, he reloaded, then returned the gun to its holster. 'Right, let's give this another try.' He kicked the door as hard as he could near the lock. At first it didn't move, but with the second kick a huge crack appeared, and with the third the door burst wide open, revealing a dark back alley.

Minutes after the exit door had been broken open, Haller let the black man's body fall to the floor of the auditorium in a limp heap. He'd heard the gunshots moments before, but in the frenzy that had overcome him he had almost blanked them out. Now he was able to concentrate, and almost immediately he knew something was wrong. He sniffed and picked up smells from outside, smells that were nowhere near as strong minutes before. *No*, he thought. *No!* He leaped back up onto the stage and ran through the door into the workshop. He could feel a breeze now too. The other man had obviously escaped. Haller had wasted time, let his guard down, and now he was paying the price. *Damn!* He entered the boiler room carefully, despite the urgency of the situation. The man he was dealing with wasn't stupid. He wasn't beyond setting traps. But, as it turned out, he had indeed gone.

Haller kicked the spent bullet clips across the floor and grunted at the mess the man called Mason had made of the door. He stood in the open doorway for a few silent seconds, anger boiling inside him. This wasn't supposed to happen. No one was meant to get out. He felt an overwhelming urge to throw his head back and howl, but that wasn't a good idea. He would now have to hunt the man down outside. That would mean keeping to shadows, using his nose constantly to stay on the man's trail. And there were so many smells out there. It was going to be difficult.

The wind changed direction momentarily, and stopped blowing into the room. In that interval Haller picked up a familiar scent. The chemical smell. The smell he'd been tracking before the interruption. The smell that had been hiding something. Had someone else been in there all along? Had he helped Mason escape? He inhaled the smell again. Maybe this was a good thing. Maybe it would make Mason easier to track. He stepped out of the building and into the alley, moving forward cautiously, sniffing for danger, and the scent of his prey.

11: LURE OR REPEL

They didn't stop until they were on the main road, just along from Al's Express Mart. Mason was panting and holding his side.

'How is it?' Gerontius looked at the red patch that had spread across to the front of the man's shirt.

'I'll live.'

'You should go to a hospital.'

'No – there are more important things to deal with right now. I've got to get to the bottom of this mess, find out who's responsible. Look' – he put a hand on the boy's shoulder – 'go home. Go home and try and forget about all this, OK? If that's possible.'

'Won't that thing come after me?'

'It's me it wants. There's a chance I might be able to stop it if I can determine whether it was sent after us.'

'Sent after you?' A bus shot past. The jaw of one of the passengers dropped open as he saw the blood on Mason's shirt.

'Yeah. As crazy as it sounds, I think that thing might have been hired to kill my friends and me.'

'But it's a monster.'

'Yeah, I know.'

'Is there anything I can do?'

'No. Look, you shouldn't have been dragged into this in the first place.'

'But what if it—?'

'Listen, let me deal with it. It's my problem.'

'But you don't deserve this.'

Mason wondered whether maybe he *did* deserve it. Maybe he had brought all this upon himself. The Knightsbridge bank job had been his responsibility, and it had gone wrong. Any retribution from Slaughter was down to his failure. He tried to smile despite the pain in his side. 'It doesn't matter whose fault it is. I just need to put things right, you know?'

Gerontius wasn't sure he did, but he nodded anyway. Traffic passed them as they tried to decide what to do next.

'Look,' Gerontius said. 'I live at thirty-three Stevenson Road if you need help.'

Mason looked around, trying not to laugh. What help could a teenager give him? 'You're a good kid, Gerry. Your parents must be proud of you.'

'They're dead,' Gerontius replied, looking at his feet. 'I live with my aunt and uncle.'

'Oh . . . sorry. Look, you get back home right now, OK? Leave the worrying to me.'

Unable to think of anything else to say, Gerontius nodded and turned towards the bus that was now approaching the stop. It was past four thirty so Leah would have finished her shift, and was probably on her way home. He boarded and sat down, looking out of the window. But Mason had gone.

* * *

Haller crept along a small side road; it was deep in shadow and provided him with more than enough cover. He turned and climbed the wall to his left, then dropped down into the storage yard of one of the shops on the main road. He had to negotiate several more walls and fences before he found himself at the back of Al's Express Mart. The men had been there earlier – he'd seen them. And there was always a chance that Mason would retrace his steps. He skulked for a while, trying to focus on the sounds from the shop. He could hear what sounded like three voices. One of them was a West-Indian lady, another a young girl and the third a middle-aged man. From what he could hear, the man was a customer, not Mason as he'd hoped. But that didn't mean Mason wasn't there, hiding. He gritted his teeth and let out a growl of discomfort as his damaged eye socket contorted and began rebuilding itself. It was already burning and itching madly, and the pain was likely to get worse before it got better. The bullet had hit the bone above his eye but luckily hadn't penetrated the brain. He continued waiting in the darkness of the yard until he heard the bell ring above the door at the front of the shop, and the customer leave. Then he made his move.

The back door was unlocked. He crept inside the building and paused for a few seconds just to make sure there were no other customers. It sounded clear. Apart from the woman singing to herself and the muffled drone of the traffic outside, there was silence. He was in a stock room not much larger than a garage, but the space was crammed with foodstuffs. There were layers upon layers of strong fragrances, mainly herbs and spices, all assaulting him at once and affecting his concentration. Padding softly to the door, he took hold and pulled the handle. The door swung slowly inwards with only a faint creaking sound. As he passed through the small kitchen area, he was hit once more by the chemical smell. This time it was overpowering, cloying. He padded over to the small cupboard underneath the sink. Opening the cupboard with one paw, he saw the almost empty bottle of Devoida, still wet from where the liquid had spilled down the side. This was it. This was the maddening smell that had been bothering him. Out of the three men, Mason was the only one he hadn't met face to face. The other two hadn't carried the smell with them, so it must be Mason. And yet Haller had been sure that Mason's scent and the chemical smell were mutually exclusive . . . What the hell was going on? He shook his head and turned round. There was no time for this – Mason could be close by.

Leah gave another bored sigh. She'd agreed to stay on for a couple of hours to serve in the shop while Hortense continued with the stocktake. She wanted to go home though. She picked up the remote control and was about to turn the television back on when she heard the door creak open at the back of the shop. From where she stood behind the counter she could see Hortense with her clipboard; she was singing softly. From her expression it looked like she hadn't heard anything. The phone started ringing, but Leah ignored it. Leaving the counter, she walked over to the centre aisle, where she could look all the way down to the storeroom door. There was nothing there. She was about to shrug off the strange feeling when she heard Hortense gasp in surprise. At once she knew that someone was in the shop. Someone who shouldn't be.

Haller knew exactly where she was from her scent. And he could sense every time she moved by the way her scent increased and decreased in strength. He doubted she'd heard the door open – she would surely have come to investigate. He turned and started creeping down the aisle towards Hortense, as soundless as only an accomplished predator could be. She still had her back to him as he approached, and her arms were in front of her, as though she was holding something . . .

Hortense stopped what she was doing. What made her stop was the smell. A waft of something wet, canine perhaps. She took a deep breath and wheeled round.

'Oh my Lord!' What she saw defied belief. At first she thought it was a large dog – the way it was tensed on all fours like that, but . . . it was wearing clothes! She stared it in the eye, then followed the creature's gaze as it moved to the clipboard she was holding in her shaking hands. She looked at it too, then decided to put it to some use.

'You beast! Get away! Get away now!' All horror drained from her: she swung the metal clipboard and caught the monster hard on the head. It howled, fell backwards, then scrambled about on the floor, trying to get back on its feet. She advanced on it, holding the clipboard higher this time, ready to mete out more damage. 'I don't know what you're supposed to be, but you're getting out of this shop!'

'Oh my God!' Leah was behind her now, staring in disbelief at the drooling monstrosity. Behind her the phone stopped ringing. The shop was quiet, until Hortense grunted and swung her checklist once more.

This time Haller avoided the unusual weapon and bared his teeth, snarling his displeasure. He looked from the woman to the girl, noting their fear. Then he was off, back down the side aisle and out of the door to the stock room. By the time Hortense reached the back yard he was nowhere to be seen. She closed the door and locked it, then did the same with the stock room. She gave Leah a stern glance.

'I'm calling the police. You lock that door – don't let anyone in until they arrive.'

Leah stood still, trying to process what she had just seen. 'Did you . . . ? Did you see . . . ?'

'Yes, I saw it, girl! Now lock that door before it comes back.'

Leah looked at the front door almost absently. Something Gerontius had said about his parents' death had always bothered her. Something weird. And now she thought she knew what that something was.

'I have to get home,' she said.

'What?' Hortense asked, the handset already to her ear. 'You're going nowhere, young lady, until—'

'I'll be fine.' And before Hortense could stop her, Leah was out of the door, onto the street and rushing towards the bus stop.

A couple of back yards away, Haller was wincing as the pain in his eye returned. He inhaled several deep breaths through his nose and concentrated. Incredibly, he caught the chemical smell on the wind. He could tell from its direction that it wasn't coming from the shop. Was Mason closer than he thought? He sniffed again, but the strength of the odour was fading. Mason's scent had been all but consumed by the other street smells: people, litter, food, cosmetics, urine. But that other smell was so distinct. Perhaps if he followed it, it would lead him to his prey. And if someone else was involved, someone who had helped Mason escape . . . God help them. He scaled the wall to his left, then dropped into a dark loading bay that belonged to a grocer's shop. Following the chemical smell would be difficult: it meant skulking around in more alleys, side streets and back yards. But if he changed back into human form, his sense of smell would be far weaker, almost useless. He climbed onto a stack of crates and swung himself over a high fence. The scent was still moving, and he would have to work hard to keep up.

The scrap yard was nearly a mile away, but Mason decided to walk. He briefly considered phoning Slaughter again, then realized it might be a bad idea. If Slaughter really had arranged to have him killed, and knew that he was still alive, he wouldn't hang around at the yard for him . . . unless he intended to finish the job himself. Using public transport was a bad idea with his blood-soaked shirt. He moved as fast as he could, wanting to get to the bottom of the matter as soon as possible. Cain could have been right about Slaughter setting them up, but it was still too early to make assumptions. Maybe someone else had paid to have them killed. Maybe the creature was working on its own, though that seemed unlikely. One way or another, Slaughter would help resolve the matter. And if it turned out that he was behind the hit, he'd pay. They'd been friends for a long time, but if the boss had ordered his death, neither the friendship nor Slaughter himself would survive the night.

According to his watch it was a quarter to five. It was hard to believe they'd been in the theatre so long. It had all happened so fast. The road beside him was packed with early rush-hour traffic. Drivers beeped their horns and vocalized their urgency to return to the comfort of their own homes. People pushed impatiently past each other to get into the Goldhawk Road tube station, hearing their train approach. Mason pressed the wound in his side to see if it was still bleeding. It seemed to have stopped. *Thank God.* He'd removed the sliver of wood without much care, hoping it wouldn't do further damage. Apart from the occasional flash of pain and shortness of breath, everything seemed OK. He crossed the road, weaving through the slow-moving vehicles, and turned into a side street. With few people around, he picked up the pace and jogged to the end of the long road, where he took a left turn. About fifteen minutes later he turned onto Garnier Road, and a short way down found the scrap yard dark and deserted.

Slaughter had gone – not that Mason was entirely surprised. He walked towards the portakabin just to make sure there was no one about. On the door he noticed a small yellow note that had been stuck at eye level with clear tape.

H
Have left early on a personal matter. Come by tomorrow
at ten a.m.
S

Was H the monster? Or was it someone else Slaughter had been doing business with? Either way, Mason wasn't going to get the answers he wanted tonight. He couldn't go after Slaughter at home with all the family around. And if he wasn't home, he could be anywhere. Mason swore openly. Then, looking up, he saw the reflection of a figure in the window, approaching him silently from the darkness of the scrap yard.

The bus had dropped Gerontius off near home, and he'd run the rest of the way. All the lights were off in the house. Leah wasn't in, so he'd phoned the shop but had received no reply. Where was she?

He paced around for a while, then phoned Leah's friend Mandy to see if she was there. No luck. He decided to wait a while longer before panicking. Upstairs he showered, taking care to remove all the chips of wood from his hair, then changed into clean clothes.

He had just sat down on the sofa to start thinking through all that had happened, when Leah arrived. He rushed to the front door and Leah jumped as she saw him standing right in front of her.

'You're not going to believe what happened,' she said quickly, closing the door behind her. 'Are you all right?' she asked, reading the troubled expression on his face.

'I need to tell you something,' Gerontius replied. 'Something I've never told anyone. About what happened to Mum and Dad.'

Leah said nothing for a second or two, then: 'It wouldn't have anything to do with werewolves, would it?'

Gerontius's expression changed from one of gloom to shock. 'How did you . . . ?'

'Go and sit down. I'll make us a cup of tea. We could both do with it.'

He leaned forward with his hands clasped together, trying to work out where in the story to begin. Leah sat on the armchair with her legs folded beneath her, holding her mug of tea and gazing at Gerontius through the wisps of steam.

'I agreed to stay late at the shop while Hortense did the stocktake.' She looked down into the mug, as if seeing the events that had transpired in its depths. 'I heard something come in through the stock-room door so I went to have a look. It was . . . I couldn't believe it. It was a bloody—'

'Did it touch you?' Gerontius was shaking slightly.

'No. Hortense hit it with her clipboard and it took off.'

'It was probably looking for him.'

'Who?'

'Mason. You remember those three guys in suits that were in the shop earlier talking to Hortense? He was one of them. I think that thing was hunting them. That's why I was gone for so long. I was with them in this theatre. I think it meant to trap them in there.'

'The werewolf?'

'Yeah. Mason thought it might have been hired to kill them – I don't know why, but—'

'That's just crazy,' Leah said, sipping her tea.

'Yeah, it is.'

'I always thought there was something strange about what happened to Uncle Harry and Aunt Nadia . . .' She looked across at her cousin, knowing this would be hard on him. 'You don't have to talk about it if you don't want to, but . . .'

'It's OK.' It really was tough. Just mentioning them brought back the tingling feeling in his eyes that threatened tears. But he had to do it. If not now then eventually. 'You know I said Mum and Dad were killed by—'

'Wolves?'

'Yeah, well, it wasn't.'

'It was that thing?'

'Yeah . . .' Gerontius looked up at her. 'Not long before the crash we stopped at a shop along the road to get something to drink. There was an old man there, and when we

101

left, he tried to warn us about it. At the time we thought he was just mad . . .'

As the memory of that afternoon came seeping back, he wished he could go back in time, back to a point when he and his parents were together . . .

12: WARNING

His mum spotted it first.

'Hey, let's stop over there for a drink or something.'

'Where?'

'That little shack up ahead.'

'Oh yeah. Hey! You in the back,' his dad called over his shoulder. 'You awake?'

'Mm,' Gerontius mumbled in reply.

'You want anything to drink? An ice cream?'

'Ice cream? It's freezing outside,' Gerontius said, rubbing the condensation from the window with the sleeve of his sweater and making himself a small viewing hole.

'So?'

'Can I have a can of lemonade?'

'Lemonade? Any particular brand, or just generic?'

'Huh?'

Harry Moore pulled into the small area in front of the wooden building and parked. 'You coming in with us?'

'Nah.' But then he thought about it, and realized it might be his only chance to get out of the confines of the small car for miles. 'Oh, all right, I'll come.' He opened his door and stepped out into the cold air. His mother appeared by his side, hooked her arm through his and walked with him towards the shop.

'Bet you wish you'd brought your camera now, eh?'

'Yeah,' Gerontius replied dryly. 'I could have hundreds of pictures of trees and snow by now.'

'Oh, don't be such a misery-guts,' she said, tugging on his arm. 'We'll be at the next town soon. There'll be lots of interesting things to see there.'

I bet there won't, he thought.

Inside the small shop they bought bottles of water and lemonade, handing the money over to a large man with a long white beard. When they stepped outside, another man had appeared, sitting on the bench in front of the building. He was smoking a roll-up cigarette, his right hand resting on a large rifle that lay across his lap. He seemed to be staring off into space, but as they passed him, his head snapped in their direction and he jumped up. Seeing nothing but the rifle at that point, the three of them stopped and stood still. The man's hair was mainly black, as was his beard, though the odd line of grey could be seen. There were at least three scars on his face, one of them jagged.

'You are British?' he asked. The rifle, though tilted towards the ground, was still pointing in their direction.

Harry, trying to diffuse the tension of the situation, replied easily, 'That's right. We're on holiday. Just driving through.' He put his hands on the shoulders of his wife and son, smiling at the older man as he started to lead them away.

'Wait,' the man said, walking after them. Although in appearance he was strong and healthy, he seemed exhausted, as though he hadn't slept for some time. 'Listen to me!' He continued to follow them.

Although he didn't want to, Harry stopped and turned back to face the armed stranger, not wanting to upset him.

'This area is bad. There are very bad things here – you understand me?'

'Bad, yes. I understand.' He smiled a little more than was strictly necessary.

'No! You don't understand!' The man seemed angry now. What the hell was up with him? Gerontius looked at the car, which now seemed less boring and claustrophobic than it had a few minutes ago. 'You have not seen what is out there,' the man went on, gesturing towards the wide expanse of forest ahead of the car. 'You must stay in your vehicle. You must not get out.'

'OK,' Harry replied. 'Thanks very much.' He turned back to the car, his key at the ready. 'I thought this was Austria, not the bloody safari park.'

'Why?' Gerontius asked the stranger, unable to contain his curiosity.

'Shh!' Harry put the key in the lock and opened the door. Nadia was already by the passenger side. Gerontius stayed where he was, dying to know what it was the man was warning them about. The fellow approached him.

'Come on, Gerry, we need to get going,' Harry said.

The stranger looked from Gerontius to his father and

back again. 'There is a terrible beast out there. If it smells you . . . it will hunt you.'

Nadia and Harry were feeling more anxious now. Gerontius was fascinated though.

'What sort of a beast? A wolf?'

'Wolf?' In the old man's thick Austrian accent, the 'w' in wolf was pronounced as a 'v'. He laughed. 'No, not wolf. Wolves are nothing to fear – they do not hunt men.'

'So what is it then?' Harry sighed audibly; he was losing his patience now.

'It is perversion of the wolf! A hybrid!' The man leaned closer to Gerontius now. 'Of all things man has done to the animals of this world, this is worst!'

'Are you . . . ? Are you talking about werewolves?' If Harry hadn't thought the man crazy already, he did now.

'It is hunting season,' the man said, looking Harry in the eye. 'But not for men.'

Just then the owner of the shop walked out, his arms crossed. 'Hans,' he called, betraying a note of concern. 'Your coffee, it is cold.'

Hans mumbled something in reply, then, turning, added one last thing: 'Young man . . . some monsters have a good and a bad side – and it is easy to confuse them. You see?' Gerontius wasn't sure he did. 'Man is the cruellest animal.' And with that Hans turned and walked back towards the hut.

'Come on, Gerry,' Nadia said. 'Get in.'

In seconds they were moving again, and Gerontius was falling asleep once more, lulled into slumber by the sound of the engine. *Werewolves*, he thought, as he drifted off. *Wouldn't that be cool . . .*

Gerontius continued telling the story, reliving the moment when the creature landed on the car, causing his father to swerve and roll the vehicle off the road. When he reached the part where he found the creature feasting on his parents' bodies, he hesitated, and was only able to finish after some reassurance from his cousin. When the tale was over, he sat back on the sofa feeling drained and tortured. Leah looked at the mug beside her, the tea in it now cold.

'I knew something wasn't right. I knew wolves didn't attack people. And whenever anyone asks you about your parents, you always look more afraid than sad, like something's still out to get you.'

'Yeah, and I was right. It is!'

'But you said it was after that Mason guy and his friends.'

'Yeah, but it might have seen me in the theatre . . . It might remember me.'

'It was eight years ago though – and in Austria. How could it possibly be the same one? And here in London . . .'

'But how many people do you think have seen one werewolf, let alone two?' asked Gerontius.

'Look, never mind that.' Leah came and sat down next to him on the sofa. 'It can't find us now, can it?'

'I hope not. Mason might come here though. I told him to if he needed help.'

'What? Are you mad?'

'He helped me get out. He saved my life.'

'But that thing could follow him here!'

'Nah, he knows what he's doing. He'd only come if it was safe.'

Haller was closing in on the scent now. The man must have stopped. Turning a corner into a quiet residential street, he negotiated a small brick wall and landed softly in the front garden of a modest semi-detached house. He padded carefully along, keeping below the front hedge, and slipped effortlessly over the next wall into another property. A few houses later, the smell became overpowering, and returning cautiously to the street, he took a good sniff of the night air. It was so close now. He crept round the back of a white van and pushed his face up against one of the rear windows. It was dark inside but he could just make out the shape of a bucket, a blanket and what looked like a smashed bottle. A smashed bottle that, according to the soggy label, had at one time contained Devoida disinfectant. *No!*

Haller wanted to scream aloud, or howl, or both. But neither would have done him any good. He gritted his teeth and shook in anger. He'd fooled himself. Followed the wrong trail. The only thing to do now was to return to the scrap yard and hope that Mason had gone there looking for Slaughter. He hoped the boss wasn't there, because if he was he might want to know why Haller hadn't finished the job. But maybe there was still time to tie things up, if he could get back there before Mason. He turned, and making sure there was no one in sight, bounded back down the street.

Mason wasn't sure about drawing his gun. If it was just a passer-by being nosy, things could get unnecessarily messy. Then again, if he didn't draw his gun, he could end up dead. He hated decisions like this. He turned round, trying to look casual, and pretended to be surprised to find the man standing there.

'Oh! Sorry, you made me jump there, mate. Excuse me.' He made to walk past the strange-looking man, but was stopped by a hand on his arm.

'Please. We must talk.' The man spoke with a German accent.

'I'm sorry?' Mason looked at the rough, scarred hand, then up at the similarly scarred face.

The other man released his grip. 'We must talk. You are being hunted.'

'I'm what?' How the hell did this guy know? Unless . . . Mason did draw his gun now, pointing it at the other man's forehead. He moved round in an arc, keeping the man in his sights all the while, until his back was against a large wrecked truck. 'Who are you? Make any sudden movements and I'll shoot. Understand?'

The other man merely smiled. He was a good deal older than Mason – sixty perhaps, maybe older. He had a short grey-black beard. Curls of hair stuck out from under the brim of his small, faded brown hat. Even under all the clothes the man was wearing, Mason could tell that he was well built.

'There is no time for confrontation,' the man said, still smiling.

'Then answer me. Who are you?'

'My name is Hans. I am seeking the one that hunts you. I must locate the beast before it is too late.'

'The wolf?' Mason watched the man's face, trying to read as much as he could.

'It is no wolf, my friend. It is an abomination. It spends most of its time in human form, but when it needs to fight, to kill, it changes into the beast.'

'Where does it come from?'

'Austria. Where I am from also. I have tracked it for a very long time but have only caught up with it on three occasions. It is very elusive. I must destroy it tonight while I have the chance, and before it exposes itself too much. Can you imagine what would happen if everyone found out that werewolves existed? It must be stopped now. Perhaps we should work together to accomplish this.' The man was calm. He didn't seem too bothered by the weapon Mason was pointing at his face.

'How did you know it was tracking me? How do I know *you're* not that thing?'

'To answer your first question, I've been following it for quite some time. I knew it had been in this area, because I caught sight of it by accident earlier this afternoon. I lost it near here, but when I came to this junk yard I found evidence of it marking its territory. The urine of a werewolf is very distinct. I can show you, if you would like.'

'No thanks.'

'Well then, in answer to your second question: if I were the beast, I'd have killed you by now.'

'Really?' Mason considered this, then lowered his gun. 'Well then, I guess I should thank my lucky stars you're not. Why don't you tell me everything you know about this thing?'

'It was a man once,' Hans said, sitting on the top step by the door to the cabin. 'Just like us. But at some point it was bitten by a beast.'

'How many are there?'

'As far as I know there have been three. This is the third.'

'Where's the first?'

'The first was killed.'

'By you?'

'No – by my . . . predecessor, you might say.'

'Right,' Mason said, leaning against the truck and holstering his gun. 'What about the second one?'

'The second one is also dead. Killed, I think, by the third.'

'It killed one of its own?'

'*Ja.* I think by nature it prefers to work alone. It is not a pack animal like the wolf. It does not desire company. When there are two together, there could be rivalry.'

'So the third one was bitten by the second?'

'*Ja*, and the curse was transferred via the bite.'

'So this third one is the only one alive? How do you know there aren't more out there?'

'Well, *ja*, there might be, but I am only interested in this line. The original – it slaughtered many members of my family. I will not stop until the bloodline is severed.'

'So how is it able to talk and think like a man?'

'Because it has the mind of a man,' Hans replied, taking a small metal case from an inside pocket of his long, worn coat. He opened it and produced a short black cigarette, pushing it into one corner of his mouth. He offered the case to Mason but he declined. With the cigarette lit, Hans continued. 'The body is half man, half wolf. In that, the animal part has no say. But in the mentality it is all human.'

'What?' Mason wasn't sure he understood. 'It's half wolf in body – but not in mind?'

'*Ja*. You see, the wolf is neither good nor evil. It kills because it must – to feed. It does not hunt for sport, for pleasure. That is not the wolf's way. Only human beings suffer from emotional instability. If you say a wolf is a sadist, you may as well say a deer is a masochist. If you get my meaning.'

'So it's the human part of this thing that makes it dangerous?'

'The werewolf is an enhancement of the man, but a bastardization of the wolf.' He locked eyes with Mason again. 'Never forget this.' He inhaled on the cigarette and blew a plume of thick smoke up into the night sky. 'And it's what the victim does with that enhancement that defines him as a man.'

'Right,' Mason said, feeling overwhelmed by the information he'd been given. 'So how does that help us kill this thing?'

'You will see.'

'Well, you're not going to find it sitting there, are you? Shouldn't we be tracking it or something?'

'No need,' Hans replied, before taking another deep pull on the cigarette.

'And why's that?'

'Because it'll be here very soon.'

13: ORIGINAL WEREWOLF

'I guess the best thing to do now is go somewhere public where it wouldn't want to be seen.' Gerontius was looking out of the window again.

'Like where?' asked Leah.

'I dunno,' he replied. 'Cinema, the underground, a hospital . . .'

'A pub?'

'We're not going to a pub.'

'Why not?'

'Because we'd draw attention to ourselves. We're too young to be in pubs anyway.'

'What? I've been to pubs with Mandy and her brothers loads of times. We lived above one until recently, remember?'

'Yeah, I know, but we need to go somewhere we can blend in, and where there are a lot more people.' Gerontius paced around the living room. Leah had turned the television on but kept the volume low. It was comforting in a way, like a third person. 'We could go to the police station.'

'Nah, they'd chuck us out,' Leah said. 'We'd need a reason to be there, and we could hardly tell them the truth.'

'Yeah, I suppose so.'

'Have a think about it,' she said, getting up. 'I'll be back in a sec.'

'Why, where are you going?'

'Call of nature?'

'Oh, right. Sorry.' He sat back down on the sofa as her footsteps sounded on the stairs, and looked at the television screen. The news had just started. He wondered how long it would take for the monster's work to make the headlines. Just then the phone rang. It was a chilling sound. The monster couldn't possibly have known his number, and even if it had, why would it want to ring him? Perhaps it was Mason. Could he have found his number and called to see if he was OK? He picked up the handset and put it to his ear, waiting a second or two before answering.

'Hello?'

'Oh . . . hi, Gerry, is Leah there?' It was Mandy, Leah's best friend.

Gerry thought before answering, wondering how much he should tell her. 'Hi, Mand. Leah's not here at the moment, I'm afraid.'

'Really? Oh. Can you get her to call me?'

'Actually, she has to work late tonight, so I'm not sure . . . I can get her to call you in the morning, if that's OK?'

'No, don't worry, I'll call her at work.'

'Oh, she'll be doing the stocktake. Might be best to let her get on with it, you know?'

'Right, OK . . . I'll just send her a text then,' Mandy replied, sounding a little disappointed.

'Thanks – bye.' Gerontius hung up just as Leah came back down the stairs.

'Who was that?' she asked.

'Mandy. Told her you were at work and not to disturb you. Best not to get anyone else involved.'

'I suppose . . . although . . .'

'What?'

'Well, why don't we go over to her house? I mean, we don't have to tell her anything, but we'd be safe over there. That thing wouldn't try and attack us with other people around.' She leaned against the door frame, crossing her arms.

'No, it's not safe enough. We need crowds of people. We don't want to put her in danger either. We have to go where it won't attack us.'

'It won't know where Mandy's is.'

'No, but it could follow us there.'

'It could follow us anywhere then.'

'Yeah, I know,' Gerontius said. 'That's why we need to choose the place carefully.'

'All right. Where do you suggest?'

Instead of going straight to the scrap yard like he'd planned, Haller first went back to the theatre to remind himself of Mason's scent. Having his smell in his nostrils would help him locate the man, whether he was at the scrap yard or not. Thankfully the man's scent was still strong. He took a series of long, deep snorts, ensuring that the scent was burned into his memory, then rushed back out of the fire exit and onto the road. It was incredible to think that he'd allowed Mason to escape. Especially after he'd killed the other two so easily. He'd been so pitifully close to completing the job.

He picked up Mason's scent trail near the main road, as he'd expected. He must have headed back to the scrap yard after all. Crossing the main road wasn't going to be easy, especially during rush hour. In a dark corner of an empty garage he changed back into human form, every part of him shrinking, retracting, receding. When he was finished, he rolled his head and flexed his muscles. His bones ached. He tucked his baggy shirt in and buttoned up his long dark overcoat to hide, as best he could, the bullet holes and blood stains. Then he strode out into the busy street. He would cross over, find a nice quiet side road, then change back again. He wasn't used to changing so many times in such a short space of time. He hoped it wouldn't cause any problems.

'You seem remarkably relaxed,' Mason said, wondering why he was waiting around with this stranger, possibly inviting his own death. 'Are you sure you can kill it? I saw it take several bullets today, almost without flinching.' He looked around the scrap yard: was the thing already out there, watching them?

'I can kill it,' Hans replied, flicking the cigarette butt through the air. 'But it won't be easy. It is very strong and resourceful. Only its brain and heart are vulnerable, and they must be destroyed completely to ensure death.'

'So a few well-placed bullets can do it?'

'*Ja.*'

'Do they have to be silver?'

'Ha! No. High-calibre rounds, fired at close range, are best. Dumdum and cross-cut bullets are good if you want maximum damage. A shotgun is a good choice too. It will wind it long enough for you to get close and fire another shot into the right area. It's best to do it while he's in human form too, then it is more difficult for him to heal. But the hardest part is getting the opportunity, you see? It is not going to stand still and let you take aim. It is a moving target.'

'Have you fought it before?'

'*Ja*. Three times.'

'And how did it go?'

'It still breathes,' Hans replied, raising his eyebrows. 'All I have to show for my troubles are scars.'

'I wish that's all *I* had. I've lost two friends today. I don't know what I'm going to tell their families.' Mason stared up into the night sky. 'You know what? I think I'll hang around. That's if you don't mind.'

'It is fine by me,' Hans replied, sniffing the air.

Mason turned and leaned against the side of the cabin. 'So, do you know much about the first werewolf? Like where it came from?'

'All I know is a tale, passed down through generations. Some believe it, some don't. I do. Because as wild as it is . . . it makes a kind of sense. It happened sometime in the middle of the nineteenth century, near a town called Holzgau in Austria. A young man, Peter, was accused of witchcraft by the other townspeople, so his father punished him by sending him into the nearby woods to kill one of the wolves that had been feeding on the livestock. That night, while wandering through those very woods, Peter came upon some wolf scat.'

'Scat?'

'*Ja*, droppings.'

'Oh, right.'

'He also found the body of a deer that had been half eaten. He knew therefore that wolves were nearby. And sure enough, as he was leaving the clearing, he heard something approach, so he raised his rifle and turned to face it.'

'A wolf?'

'It had come back to reclaim its meal. But it was ill, and it had not been able to sense the presence of the young man. When it saw him, it was startled. And this, in turn, startled Peter. I can only imagine how he must have felt, seeing those eyes like burning suns. But the wolf only wanted its food, so it picked up the carcass in its mouth and started to back away out of the clearing. Unfortunately, Peter lost his footing at that moment, and as he slipped, the rifle went off. From the sound the animal made, he knew he had hit it.

'At first he felt guilty. But, realizing he'd done what he'd set out to do, his feelings soon changed. He reached down to touch the wolf, to feel its coat for the first time. He had not expected the animal to be so big and couldn't help but admire it. But he soon realized that something was wrong. He could see a strange green colour in its eyes and in the tongue that flopped from its mouth. Then, to Peter's horror, the wolf lifted its head and clamped its jaws onto his arm. He screamed and tried to shake the arm free, but the wolf wouldn't let go. In the end he had to fire the rifle using only his other arm, the bullet passing through the animal's brain, killing it instantly. Peter got to his feet and stood over the body, unsure whether he wanted to take it back to town or leave it where it was. Then, while he was still pondering his choices, a wave of nausea consumed him, and he fell unconscious.

'When he awoke, he was lying under a different tree, in another part of the forest. His clothes had gone, as had the rifle and the body of the wolf. He walked up the hill until he could stand and survey the valley. He was now some miles from where he had fallen, with no memory of the journey. And as he began to fear for his mind, he heard sounds around him. A wolf pack. Peter was terrified at first, but soon the fear turned to rage. The illness inside him reacted with his emotions, and his body changed. The wolves could only watch as the boy became something horrible. Confused and terrified, they fled, leaving Peter to come to terms with what had happened to him.' Hans took out the cigarette case and opened it.

'What then?' Mason was touching the wound in his side again. The pain had returned.

'He went back to his father, who had been waiting anxiously for his return, feeling guilty for sending him into the forest alone. The next morning one of the townspeople found the man's body impaled on a fence post. His bones had been crushed and his face nearly torn off.'

'Jesus. Did his father become a werewolf too?'

'No. His father was killed during the assault. To become a werewolf, you must survive the attack and live long enough for the curse to take hold. Then the body starts to rebuild itself.'

'But how could he just kill his father like that?'

'Peter was very quick to exploit his new strength. There was a darkness in him all along. This was his chance to do what he wanted without anyone being able to stop him. The curse removed his inhibitions, gave him powers he had only dreamed of. It fuelled the terrible evil that was always in his heart. You see, wolves – they are wild but innocent. They are incapable of man's malice, his cruelty. That's why they hate the werewolf. Why they fear it. If the curse is passed to an evil soul, then only the worst things can happen.'

'I guess it gives wolves a bad name.'

'*Ja.*'

'But the one that's here is the third werewolf?'

'By my reckoning. I have found no evidence to suggest there are more in this line.'

'And does it know that you're here? That you've followed it?'

'I don't think so. I've developed ways of masking my scent. It's the only real advantage I have. It is coming here because it has your scent in its head, and you have done nothing to disguise it.'

'Well, shouldn't I do something?'

'It is already too late. Besides, if you cover your scent

with something else now, it will know what you have done and just follow the new smell.'

'Great. But what about the boy?'

'What boy?'

'He was with me in the theatre. What if the creature goes after him?'

'No!' Hans stood up. 'Why didn't you tell me about this?'

'I—'

'Where is the boy now?'

'At home, I think. He gave me his address.'

'Go! Go now! It should be on its way here after you, but just in case it has followed this boy, you should go and protect him. The beast will not allow witnesses. It will eliminate all those who see it in its changed form. Take the boy somewhere with a lot of people. The scents will confuse it. Go on, do it! I will stay here.'

'You're sure you can kill it?' Mason started off towards the road.

'I am.'

'You haven't managed it yet.'

'No, but I have a good feeling about tonight.'

'Really?'

'*Ja*,' Hans lied. 'Really.'

14: A Special Kind of Dog

Gerontius peered through the gap in the curtains. It was quiet outside and no one seemed to be around. But the creature could be out there. It could be watching him right now. He let the curtains fall back into place.

'So we need to be safe until morning?' Leah had sat down again.

'Yeah.'

'Couldn't we just call the police and say that someone's trying to break in? That would get them over here.'

'No – we could be waiting for ever for them. Come on, I think we should make a move. We can get the bus at the end of the road.' Gerontius moved away from the window.

'Would it attack us out there?'

'No, not in the street. At least, I don't think so. From what I saw of it in the theatre, it seemed to be intelligent. If it thinks like a man, it probably won't take any risks.'

'Come on then, let's go.' Leah stood up, took her mug into the kitchen and poured the cold tea down the sink. Gerontius walked into the hall to get their coats.

'Gerry?'

'Yeah?' He left the coats on the banister and went through to the kitchen.

'This is nowhere near as bad as we think it is, is it?' Leah attempted a smile.

'No. Of course not.' He went over and hugged her. Lifting his head, he happened to catch movement in the garden, just beyond the glass of the back door.

'What's wrong?' Leah could tell from the way Gerontius had frozen that something wasn't right.

'There's . . .' His voice was soft, almost a whisper. 'There's something in the garden.'

He could smell rust, petrol, oil and something underneath. Yes . . . Mason had returned to the scrap yard after all. In the end, Haller's journey hadn't been as easy as he'd hoped. He'd had to change back twice after leaving the main road, just to be sure he was on the right track, and had only remained in human form once he was certain that the scent led to the scrap yard. He'd alternated between walking fast and running, knowing that time was ebbing away from him, and that the longer Mason was out of his sight the more chance there was of losing him. At one point he ran straight into a cyclist who had just emerged from a small lane. It was then that he realized he'd taken a wrong turn, and had to retrace his steps to work out where he'd lost his way. Eventually he'd reached the scrap yard: he sneaked in through a gap in the corrugated-iron fence and prowled around until he was close to the portakabin.

Crouching under the shadowy hulk of an overturned bus, he transformed and inhaled the air, listening hard at the same time for any sound that might give away the location of his quarry. Unusually Mason's scent wasn't as potent as he'd expected. But he had to be around somewhere. There was another smell that bothered him: smoke, from a cigarette. It was unusual but familiar. He hadn't detected it on Mason, or on Slaughter ... So who was it? He moved slowly from his hiding place and crept around the piles of junk until the front of the portakabin was in view.

No! It couldn't be. Not here, not now. How did he always manage to find him no matter where he went? Right now the Austrian was rolling a cigarette around in his fingers as if debating whether to smoke it or not. They'd fought in Austria, Germany and France – and now it seemed they would have to fight again. Perhaps it was time to finish this man once and for all. If something wasn't done, he would only get in the way of him completing the job. And that couldn't be allowed. Haller took another good sniff of the night air. *Shit!* Mason's scent was weakening. He must have left the scrap yard. But even though his target was getting away again, Haller couldn't fight the desire to vent his anger on the man sitting outside the cabin. He must have warned Mason, must have helped him, given him information. *This is the last time you get in my way,* Haller thought as he advanced slowly.

'Good evening,' Hans said, without even looking up. The beast that had been sneaking up on him stopped. 'You took your time, my friend. I was beginning to get bored.' He stood up and smiled at Haller, not the least bit shocked by the sight that greeted him.

Haller bared his teeth and stood up straight. He spat onto the ground. 'You chose the wrong career, Old Man,' he growled.

'Perhaps . . .' Hans put the cigarette in his mouth and lit it.

Infuriated by this, Haller roared and rushed towards him, one claw raised, ready to strike. When he was no more than a couple of metres away, the man whipped a shotgun from inside his jacket and blew a hole in the creature's stomach. Haller howled in pain as he flew backwards through the air, landing hard on the ground.

Only a mile or so away, Janice Evans was driving recklessly through the busy evening traffic. Her new partner, Mark Gould, gripped the sides of the passenger seat, certain that they were going to crash. But he didn't want to question her driving, not this early in their association, and not so soon after she'd lost her previous partner. From photographs Gould had seen what the creature had done to Talbot's body. It wasn't pretty, and he intended to do whatever was necessary to avoid a similar fate. Evans swerved round a bend and they were soon making good progress through Shepherd's Bush.

'We're nearly there,' she said, still concentrating on the traffic ahead. 'It's probably gone by now, but we should be prepared just in case.'

'In case of what?'

'In case . . .' She took her eyes off the road, causing Gould to tense and make a quiet moaning sound. 'In case it's still there.' She slowed the car to a stop in the bus lane.

'Right, come on. Look lively, and remember, don't intimate to anyone that it's a lycanthrope . . .'

'I know, I know,' Gould said, unbuckling his seat belt. 'It's a very special type of dog.'

'*Unusual*. It's an *unusual* type of dog.'

'Right, sorry. *Unusual*.'

They knocked on the glass of the door, and had to show their identification before Hortense would let them in.

'What time do you call this? I could have been killed by now.'

'We got here as fast as we could, madam – the traffic this time of—'

'I don't care about the traffic! I want protection! And why aren't you in uniform?'

'We're not regular officers, we work for the—'

'You're late! I know that much.'

'Yes, well, we're here now so—'

'It's a good job I had my clipboard or we could have been history.'

'Clipboard?' Gould took out his notebook.

'Sorry, did you say "we"?' Evans asked.

'Yes, Leah and me. Leah is the daughter of the owners. She's working here for the holidays.'

'And where is Leah now?' Evans asked, looking around the shop.

'She went home.'

'You let her go?'

'I couldn't stop her!' Hortense protested. 'She was out of the door before I had a chance.'

129

'Did she leave before or after the . . . intruder?'

'Oh, she went after he had cleared off.'

'She's probably safe then. But we'll need to pay her a visit afterwards, just to take a statement.'

'OK, I can give you her address.'

'That would be great. But first, could you show us where the intruder went?'

'Yes, I'll show you where it went. It went back outside with its tail between its legs. You wouldn't believe it if you saw it. I've heard stories about werewolves, but I didn't know they were real.'

Evans and Gould exchanged glances.

'I'm sure it wasn't a werewolf, madam,' Evans said as they followed the woman down the centre aisle.

'No,' Gould agreed. 'Just a special kind of dog.' He turned to Evans, who gave him an unimpressed glance.

'Dog?' Hortense turned to them, the key to the stock room in one hand, her trusty clipboard in the other. 'It was no dog! It was wearing clothes!'

'Well,' Gould said, trying desperately to impress his new partner, 'some people dress their dogs up, you know . . .'

'Eh?' Hortense's eyes widened. 'Listen, young man, I know a dog when I see one, and that was no dog.' She unlocked the door to the stock room. 'I locked the other door too, so if it's still around, it'll be in the back yard.' She moved forward, and as Evans rested her hand on the bulge of the gun within her jacket, she cast another disapproving glance at her new partner.

'Best let me do the talking for now.'

'People do dress dogs in clothes though,' Gould insisted, feeling like an idiot.

It felt as if he'd been hit by a car. He could hardly breathe. Looking up into the sky, he knew there might be little time left to react. With an effort he regained his feet, blood oozing from the wound in his belly as it tried to close up, leaves sticking to his damp fur.

Wham! Too late. He didn't see it coming. He flew backwards again, another blast shredding his coat and shirt at the right shoulder. He groaned. His body was being blown apart, and he didn't know if the healing process was working fast enough to mend the damage. Cold metal pellets popped out of his flesh and rolled off his body onto the floor. The cold night air whistled around him and he could feel its chill on the exposed raw flesh that moved and hissed as it mended.

The Austrian stood over him and reloaded the sawn-off shotgun. 'You are thinking what I am thinking,' he said.

'Oh yeah?' Haller coughed up blood. 'And what's that?'

'Exactly how hard' – there was a loud click as the long barrel flew back into place; the Austrian pointed the weapon directly at Haller's forehead – 'is that skull of yours?'

Wham! This time it was the Austrian's turn to fly through the air. In an instant Haller had moved his knees up and kicked out at the man before he'd had a chance to pull the trigger. Lightning fast. Something a human being would never have managed or, in this case, anticipated. Haller leaped to his feet, wincing at the pain in his abdomen, and ran as best he could over to the man lying prone on the floor. The shotgun was a metre or so away from him. Haller picked it up and, using all his strength, wrenched it apart.

The Austrian had been winded. Tears filled his eyes, but he could still make out the shape of the werewolf standing over him.

'Well,' he said, 'at least you've made the most of your abilities.' His right hand moved to his side, reaching slowly for the revolver that was holstered by his belt. There was a loud crunching sound as Haller's foot slammed down on the Austrian's hand. He screamed.

'Too slow,' commented Haller.

After he'd removed the Austrian's other weapons, he dragged him behind the office cabin, well out of view of anyone who might be passing the yard. He punched him hard and ordered him to sit against the wall.

'You're a travesty,' the Austrian said.

'Where did Mason go?' Haller asked, ignoring the comment.

'I don't know. He just left.'

'He just left?'

'*Ja.* He just left.'

Smack. The paw glanced across the Austrian's face, not doing any damage, but stunning him.

'Where . . . ?' Haller leaned closer and grabbed the Austrian's chin in one paw. 'Where did he go?'

'I'm telling you, I don't know! I was waiting here for you. When he showed up, he asked me who I was. I said I was waiting for someone. Then he just left.'

'He didn't ask who you were?'

'No – he wasn't interested. He was in a hurry.'

'Hmm.' Haller looked around and sniffed the air. Mason's scent was too strong for him to have come and gone so quickly. 'You're lying.'

'So what? You're going to kill me anyway. I can tell you what I like.'

'Really?' Haller appeared calm, in control, but he didn't have time to play games. It didn't really matter if the Austrian told him what he wanted to know or not; he'd already decided what he was going to do with him. 'I'll give you three seconds to tell me where Mason is.'

He paced in front of the man, the breath pluming visibly from his nostrils. 'One . . .' The Austrian's mouth stayed closed. 'Two . . .' He closed his eyes now. 'Three . . .' Without another word Haller picked up the Austrian, still dripping blood, raised him above his head, then brought him down hard on one knee, snapping his spine with a loud crack. 'I warned you,' he rasped.

The Austrian had no time to scream now: he was dead.

Mason remembered the name of the road. Stevenson, number thirty-three. Luckily he'd been down that way before. It took him a while to reach it though: the pain in his side seemed to be spreading, hampering his movement like a really bad cramp. Hopefully he could get it sorted out soon, maybe get some painkillers. He had to stop at one point to get his breath back and allow the pain to subside a little. As he was waiting, leaning against a wall, he heard heavy breathing in the garden behind him, like that of a large animal. He pushed himself away from the wall, feeling cold all of a sudden, and reached for his gun. There came a bark, and the head of a large mastiff bobbed into view. It stopped behind the wall and sat panting and staring at him, its head tilting quizzically to one side. Mason sighed and replaced the weapon, glancing around to check if anyone had seen him. Coast clear. *Just the Hound of the Baskervilles*, he thought. He continued on his way, wondering if he was now doomed to look over his shoulder for the rest of his life.

When he found Stevenson Road, it was dark and quiet, just like everywhere else. He located number thirty-three, opened the gate and walked up the front path. He wanted to stay out of sight as much as possible so he made for the small passage by the side of the house that led to the back garden. He had blood on his shirt and his clothes were a mess. It wouldn't do him any good to be seen like that. Lifting the latch on another, larger gate, he let himself into the back garden and crept round to what looked like the kitchen door. He peered through the mottled glass. He could make out the shape of a young girl standing by the sink, and someone else holding her. He was about to tap on the glass when a familiar shape approached.

'It's OK, it's him,' Gerontius said with relief, seeing the black and white of Mason's clothes through the distorted glass.

'*Him*? Who's *him*?' asked Leah.

134

'Mason. The guy I told you about,' he said, walking to the back door and drawing the bolt across. 'It's OK.' He opened the door and let the man in.

'Actually,' Mason said, stepping inside, 'it's not OK.'

15: IT POURS

After Gerontius had made the brief introductions, he insisted that Mason sit down so that Leah could take a look at his injury. After swallowing a couple of welcome painkillers, Mason perched on the edge of the armchair with a cup of black coffee in one hand. With the other he opened his shirt, revealing the horrible mess the huge splinter of wood had made. Leah brought a bottle of Devoida and some other items into the living room, pulling a dining chair over to where Mason sat. After she had cleaned the wound with hot water and paper towels, she opened the bottle, soaked a cotton-wool ball in the disinfectant, and began dabbing it gently around the wound.

'That stuff smells familiar,' Mason said, screwing his face up.

'Yeah,' Gerontius said. 'I've got some on my arm. I gashed my elbow running for a bus earlier. Seems like ages ago now.'

'Yeah, it's been a long day, that's for sure. You're doing a great job.' He smiled at Leah, noticing how uncomfortable she seemed. He doubted whether she was too happy about him being in the house.

'You didn't just come because of that though, did you?' Gerontius said, pointing to the injury.

'No,' Mason replied. His expression became more serious. 'When I went back to the scrap yard to talk to the boss, I met this Austrian bloke. Says he's been tracking the creature for quite some time. He's waiting there for it now. Reckons he's going to kill it.'

'Austrian?' Gerontius asked. 'Did you say Austrian?'

'Yeah.' Mason sucked in breath as the disinfectant stung.

'Sorry,' Leah said.

'What did he look like?' Gerontius asked.

'Older than me – greying beard,' Mason replied. 'Lots of scars.'

Mason took a sip of coffee then looked back over at Gerontius. 'I'm not entirely sure he can kill it though. He seemed confident, but I can't really imagine him beating that thing without one hell of a struggle.'

'At least he'll keep it away from us. Maybe it won't be able to track us now.'

'Maybe . . . but I wouldn't bet on it.'

'So it could still come after us?'

'The Austrian said that now that you've seen it, you're a threat, a witness.' Mason looked at Leah. He had to be careful what he said. He didn't want either of them to panic. 'Look, guys, don't worry, we'll all be fine provided we stay calm, OK? There are ways to beat this.'

Leah taped a bandage to Mason's side, then announced she had finished. She put all the medical things together and took them back into the kitchen.

'Top job, thank you,' Mason said. When Leah was out of earshot, he leaned closer to Gerontius, who was sitting on the arm of the sofa, and spoke softly.

'Listen, Gerry .... I'm really sorry you were dragged into this, but it might not be over yet. If that thing does find us, it'll be pretty pissed off with us for messing up its plans.'

'Yeah, I know.'

'Now, there are many good reasons why we can't go to the police. For one thing, I'm not exactly on good terms with them,' he said, patting his gun.

'At least you'd be safe.'

'Maybe,' Mason said. 'But it wouldn't do you much good. You need someone with you who knows what's going on.'

'Yeah.'

'Right, so the best thing we can do is to get ourselves somewhere safe.'

'Somewhere busy.'

'That's right. The busier the better. But I need to go home first, just for a minute, to get some things.'

'Oh, right.'

'Let's make a move then, shall we?'

'Can we get the bus to your place?'

'Yeah, I noticed there was a stop just down the street.'

'We're going,' Gerontius called out to Leah.

She came back into the living room with a questioning look on her face. 'Now?' The nervousness in her voice was obvious.

'Yeah.' Gerontius grabbed their coats from the hall. 'Look,' he said to Mason, handing Leah her red jacket. 'There could be another reason that thing wants to find me.'

'What do you mean?' Mason's brow furrowed.

'I might have seen it before. And it might have seen me before. Eight years ago.'

'Eh? What are you talking about?'

'It killed my parents.'

There was a moment or two of silence as Mason tried to process what he'd heard. He'd never imagined that events could have got any weirder. 'Are you sure it's the same one?'

'Well, I can't be certain, but . . . what if it's been after me all along and just got sidetracked with you guys?'

'Shit. It never rains but it pours.' Mason scratched his head. 'All right, come on, you can tell me about it on the way to my place.'

Leah opened the front door and Mason stepped out. As Gerontius moved past her, she whispered: 'Can we really trust this guy?'

'Yes. I promise.'

'I saw his gun – when I was cleaning him up. Who is he?'

'Look,' Gerontius said, glancing towards the front garden where Mason waited by the gate. 'He may not technically be one of the good guys, but compared to what's after us . . . we could do a whole lot worse.'

Haller could hear voices. He'd skulked in the garden for long enough, processing the scents, making sure he hadn't made a mistake. No, this was it. This was where Mason had fled. He could smell the Devoida again too. Perhaps now he could finally discover its significance. The voices he could hear were foreign – not the accents he'd been expecting. He approached the back door. It was locked. He smashed one of the glass panels with a padded paw, knowing it wouldn't make too much noise . . . Then he heard gunshots. Something wasn't right. He moved across the linoleum, his huge shoes with the custom-made holes making only slight tapping sounds as he moved. Creeping round a corner to the left, he moved into the living room, where the lights and the television had been left on. Of course. The actors on screen continued to shoot at each other, while Haller swore aloud. He turned and quickly ran upstairs, sniffing everywhere in case Mason was hiding. There were many scents, but he lingered on none of them, focusing on that of his prey and nothing else. Was this Mason's house? He hadn't pictured him as a husband or father, and this seemed to be a cosy family home. Perhaps he'd been visiting someone – relatives maybe.

He turned and followed the landing round, checking each room. Mason's scent was weaker here than downstairs. He'd only been in the house briefly, and had left perhaps minutes before Haller had arrived. This was getting tedious. In one of the small bedrooms he picked up a portable television and smashed it against one wall to vent his anger. He didn't notice the photograph on the shelf above the bed, of the boy and girl.

Hurrying back downstairs to the front door, he opened it a fraction and peered outside, listening at the same time for people nearby. A bus went past filled with passengers, most no doubt returning home from work. He couldn't hear anyone in the street. He drew in a deep breath and locked onto Mason's scent. That too now seemed mixed with the odour of that foul disinfectant, as though the two had merged at some point. What the hell was going on with that stuff? He sneaked out of the house, closing the door behind him, and moved through the front garden, then into the garden next door, keeping the scent in his nostrils all the while.

A few houses later he lost it. *Damn!* He checked that the coast was clear, then slipped onto the pavement, keeping close to the walls along the edge. He took a few good sniffs and ended up nearly banging his head against a bus shelter. He sniffed again. *You've got to be kidding!* he thought. They'd boarded a bus. He looked at the bus route and map that was framed on one side of the shelter. He would have to follow the whole route and try to determine where they'd got off. Things were spiralling out of control faster than he could have imagined.

They'd boarded the bus, bought their tickets and sat down at the back where they could talk in relative privacy. A couple of stops later Gerontius had finished telling his story. He looked down at his feet, then at Leah, who was sitting beside him. All Mason could do was stare at the boy. It was hard to believe that anyone could have survived such an ordeal, let alone an eight-year-old boy.

'Eight years ago,' he said. 'And now it's happening all over again. You poor kid.'

'It's not fair,' Leah said, to no one in particular.

'No,' Mason agreed, looking across at her. 'It isn't. But

I promise you both . . . that thing's not going to touch you.'

'You can't promise us that,' Leah said.

'I can,' he argued. 'You just wait till we get to my place.'

Twenty minutes later they were approaching Mason's stop. He stood and they followed him towards the front of the bus. The driver glanced casually across at them, and nearly swerved across the road when he saw the patch of blood on Mason's shirt.

Mason glanced down and realized how bad it looked. 'My appendix,' he said, smiling at the driver. 'I knew I should have gone private.'

The driver, not sure what to think, just nodded and brought the bus to a stop.

'Thanks,' Gerontius said as he jumped off, followed by Leah.

Mason led them about fifty metres down the steep road of old, grand houses.

'My place isn't great,' he explained. 'But we're not going to be there long, so . . .'

Leah and Gerontius exchanged glances. Leah took her cousin's arm and held him back a little.

'What's up?' he asked her.

'Are you sure about this?'

'What do you mean?'

'He's dodgy. I think we should take our chances on our own.'

'Are you kidding? He's our best hope right now.'

'But . . .' Leah had run out of arguments.

'Come on,' Gerontius assured her. 'This is the best way.'

'Yeah, but what if that thing isn't after you at all? What if it only wants him? We should get as far away from him as possible.'

'That's the problem though. We don't know what it wants . . . But if it is after me, we're better off with him.'

'I hope you're right.'

'Hey, come on!' Mason was some metres ahead now. 'It's just down here.'

'OK,' Gerontius called out. 'Come on,' he said, squeezing Leah's shoulder. 'It'll all be over soon.'

'Yeah,' she replied sullenly. 'That's what I'm worried about.'

16: SLAUGHTERHOUSE

Every time he thought he'd caught a whiff of Mason's scent, something else came along to mask it. Even if he did find the right stop, Mason's scent would probably have dissipated by then anyway. It was pointless. There had to be another way. He remembered that the lights hadn't been on in the portakabin when he'd returned to the scrap yard. Slaughter must have gone home. But Haller knew where he lived – he'd followed him back there once out of curiosity. Slaughter would know Mason's address. Even if Mason hadn't gone home yet, Haller could be there ready, waiting for him. Slaughter would be angry that he'd been let down, but there was little choice now. Mason had to die.

As he changed back into human form again, his right leg was hit by a paralysing cramp. He moaned, startling an old woman who had just turned the corner. He'd never changed this many times in one day before. It was becoming clear that it was a bad idea. He straightened his clothes and walked back over to the bus stop. Analysing the route map, he saw that there were two different buses that would take him close to Slaughter's house. If Slaughter wasn't home, things might get tricky. His family wouldn't just let him in. He was a complete stranger, and he looked a mess. But if he had to subdue them, and turn the house upside down to find Mason's address, he would. He was rapidly losing all patience and composure, but he would finish what he'd started, no matter what it took.

However, travelling on a bus was something he hated. He became irritated by the slightest of things. Passengers coughing and sneezing; children laughing; an empty bottle rolling up and down, clanking every time it hit something. He missed the forest and the solitude it afforded. But after being away from human society for so long, he'd grown curious to see if it was how he remembered it. He wondered now if he'd made the right decision. Sensing that he was being watched, he looked to his left and saw a small fair-haired boy on the seat opposite staring at him. He gave him an exaggerated smile and the child turned away, burying his head in his mother's arm. The bus was slowing down. It was his stop. He got off and walked to the end of the road, then turned into a cul-de-sac.

It was an attractive area. The houses were big, the gardens green and well-kept. Expensive cars were parked proudly in the driveways, and a sign on a nearby lamppost advised that a neighbourhood watch was in operation. Slaughter's house, naturally, was the one right at the top of the cul-de-sac, the one that looked down, or down on, the entire road. A light was on in the front room. As Haller approached, he could smell cooking. Meat. Probably beef. He was starving. If he'd been in his wolf form, the smell would have been maddening. His stomach made noises and he moaned. But he had to ignore his appetite for now. There was business to attend to. He knocked on the door and waited. He could hear a dog barking.

The door opened and a twenty-something male appeared. Immediately Haller could hear the hum of a microwave, the television in the living room, and loud rock music from upstairs. He assumed the man standing before him was Slaughter's son. There was a look of self-importance on the man's face.

'Yeah?'

'Is your dad in?'

'Yeah.' There was an odd pause.

'Well, can I see him?'

As if in answer to Haller's question the son's pocket started playing a tune. He reached inside and withdrew a small mobile phone. A blue light blinked from its fascia. He pressed a button, laughed to himself, then started to text a reply to someone.

Haller sighed. 'Sorry,' he said dryly. 'I don't want to be a nuisance . . . but could you please get your father?'

'Who wants to see him?' The son continued to text in earnest.

'I do.'

'Oh yeah? And who are you?' His right thumb danced across the buttons, his attention focused only on the phone screen, nowhere else.

'Listen,' Haller said, losing patience. 'Just tell him Haller's here to see him, and that if he keeps me waiting a minute longer I'll break his idiot son's neck.'

The son stopped what he was doing, looked up, swallowed and said: 'You'd best be careful—'

'Move!' Haller ground his teeth as the young man turned and walked hurriedly back down the hallway.

A few seconds later Slaughter himself appeared.

'You? Didn't you see the message I left?' Slaughter was clearly annoyed at Haller's appearance, but that was to be expected. 'How did you find my address?' He closed the front door behind him, not wanting his family to hear the conversation.

'That's not important, Mr Slaughter,' Haller said. 'I need Mason's—'

'Not fucking important? This is my home, you fucking numpty! All my business stays in the yard.'

'I understand – it's just that, unfortunately—'

'See me tomorrow. Now get lost before anyone sees you. Jesus.' He turned and opened the front door again. He stepped inside. 'Coming here to my house . . . You must be off your head. You're lucky I don't—'

Thud. Haller's foot blocked the door before Slaughter was able to close it. 'What the hell do you think you're doing?'

'I need Mason's address – *now*.'

'You what? Get your foot out of my fucking door! And what the hell do you want his address for anyway?'

'Because I'd very much like to kill him.'

'Eh? You mean he's still alive!' Slaughter's voice went up in pitch towards the end of the sentence, and his face went bright red. He stepped outside again. 'What the fuck happened? He should be buried by now.'

'Keep your voice down. Don't forget the neighbours.' Haller was still very calm considering the situation he was in; Slaughter, on the other hand, looked like he was approaching apoplexy.

'Fuck the neighbours! If Mason finds out I ordered him killed he'll come after me.'

'Quite right. So if you'd be kind enough to give me his address, I can go and remove that problem, so we can both sleep soundly tonight.'

'What happened today? I thought you were supposed to be a professional!'

'There were complications. Now, if you could please give me the add—' Haller was jerked forward as Slaughter grabbed him by the collar of his shirt.

'Complications? Listen, you cretin. If anything happens to me or my family, you're fucked, you understand me? I'll rain down such a storm of shit on you that—'

'Please, Mr Slaughter, this is no time for speeches—'

'Don't you get funny with me. I don't care about your reputation, if you screw me around, so help me God—'

A voice came from inside the house. Slaughter let go of Haller, looked round the door and called: 'Just a minute, sweetheart, it's business.'

'Look,' Haller said. 'We're wasting time. Tell me where Mason lives and I'll finish it.'

'All right – it's number eleven, Naughton Road. Not far from Latimer Road station. It's an old place with a black door. But you'll have to get moving – it's a few miles away.'

'Don't worry,' Haller said, turning. 'I can really move when I want to.'

'You'd better. And if Mason isn't dealt with tonight, getting paid will be the least of your worries.'

'I'll be by at ten sharp tomorrow for the money, Mr Slaughter,' Haller said, walking back down the front path. 'And if I don't get every penny that's owed, I'll give *you* something to worry about.'

'Don't you threaten me,' Slaughter roared after him. 'I'll have your fucking guts for garters!'

But Haller wasn't taking any notice. He was repeating Mason's address over and over in his head.

'I know it's not much,' Mason said, trotting down the steps to the door of the basement flat and letting them in, 'but it does its job.' He flicked on the lights. 'The family upstairs are fairly quiet. Hardly ever see them.'

A flight of steps at street level led up to a black door above. Gerontius had seen a light on behind a large bay window, but hadn't heard anything. Mason took them into the living room on the left. The walls were dirty and damp in places. The furniture looked like it had been around for generations, and the carpet was stained in a number of places. Leah looked at Gerontius as if to say, *This gets better!*

'It's all right,' he said. 'We won't be here long.'

'What?' Mason turned to him as he flicked a light on in the kitchen.

'Nothing,' Gerontius replied.

'Look, guys, if you see anything in the fridge you want,

just take it. We might have a long night ahead of us. I'm just going to get a few things from my room, then we'll be off.'

'What are we going to do?' Leah couldn't help but ask.

Mason stood there, one hand on the door frame. He looked at the floor. 'We'll have to figure that out as we go. To begin with we just need to keep moving and look for somewhere busy.' He disappeared round the corner.

Leah walked into the kitchen, followed by Gerontius, and leaned against one of the units. 'You hungry?' she asked.

'Not really.'

'Me neither. I've got butterflies. God, what's going to happen to us?'

'We'll be OK. Really. I've been thinking about it. That thing cornered those guys in the theatre because it knew that would be the easiest way to get rid of them. But since Mason escaped, things have become more difficult. He's going to be a lot harder to kill, especially if he's in a public place. The monster will have to give up, or risk being seen.'

'But it can change back into a man, can't it?'

'I don't know. I presume so – otherwise there'd be no point in it wearing those clothes.'

'If it can, it won't have to worry about people seeing it. It can get as close to us as it likes.'

'We don't know that for sure. Besides, whether it's in monster form or not, you can't just stroll up to someone in a crowd and kill them.' Leah didn't reply; she just looked at her feet, then at the kitchen window. 'Look, it could be miles away by now. It might have given up after we left the theatre.'

'But if it's the same one that killed your mum and dad . . .'

'Well, I'm not absolutely sure about that, I just . . . I saw something in its eyes, something . . .'

'If it is the same one, and it knows who you are, it'll want to get rid of you.'

'Yeah . . . That's not helping, you know.'

'Hey, guys, what's going on?' Mason reappeared wearing a new, longer coat, which seemed to be bulging in a number of places.

'Nothing,' Gerontius replied.

'All right – well, it's gone seven o'clock. The best place to go right now would be the centre of town. Piccadilly's probably the busiest place,' Mason said, picking up a map of the London tube system from the mantelpiece and ringing Piccadilly station with a pen. 'But Trafalgar Square is more open. It'd give us a better vantage point.' He ringed that station too, then stared at the map. 'It'd give us more room to manoeuvre as well.' The others just shrugged non-committally. 'All right then – until someone comes up with a better suggestion, Trafalgar Square it is.'

Gerontius followed Mason across the living room to the front door. Leah remained in the kitchen.

'Come on,' Gerontius urged.

She moved slowly towards the door. 'Can't we just stay here?'

'What?'

'I'm afraid not, sweetheart,' Mason replied. 'If that thing really can track us, it's not safe to stay here. We need to surround ourselves with other people. That way our scents will be confused, and he'll not risk attacking us with so many witnesses.'

'It's just . . . I've really gone off the idea of going back outside.'

'Believe me, it's a lot safer than in here,' Mason said, half tucking the map into his pocket.

'He's right, Leah,' Gerontius added.

She joined them by the door, reluctant to leave the flat, despite the state of it. As Mason opened the door, she looked at his coat and asked: 'Have you got more guns under there?'

'Yeah,' he replied, stepping out to make sure the coast was clear. He didn't notice the map slip from his pocket and fall to the floor. 'Don't worry, I know how to use them.' He closed the door and led them carefully up the steps, looking in both directions. All three of them were frightened that at any second something big and hideous might leap out of the shadows. Already Mason's memory had enlarged the beast, making it twice as big and terrifying as it actually was. For Gerontius the thing was as awful and evil as it had always been; Leah was still struggling to actually believe what she'd seen earlier.

They emerged onto the street and turned right. To add to their misery it was colder now, and raining. Gerontius looked across at the railings and porches of the houses opposite, wondering if something was lurking there somewhere, watching them.

'OK, we just need to go to the end of the road and hang a left,' Mason told them. 'About a hundred metres down is

Latimer Road tube station. It'll take us straight to Hammersmith, then we can get a train from there to Piccadilly Circus. We can walk to Trafalgar Square from there.'

They walked briskly away from the flat, only Mason daring to look back.

17: UNEXPECTED VISITOR

After talking to Slaughter, Haller had changed back into wolf form again, and this time the painful muscle cramps had been worse. He gave himself a few minutes to recover, then set off after Mason once more, his senses on full alert. He felt the shotgun wound in his stomach contort and finish healing, one final ball of shot popping out of the closing hole and falling into a small puddle at his feet. A single droplet of blood remained on the fur of his exposed belly, which he wiped away with one paw, spreading it across his tongue.

It was growing cold now, and it was raining. His ruined clothes and exposed fur were getting wetter by the minute, making his already aching muscles feel heavier. He'd been panting more than usual as he'd crept along the darkened roads, ducking into basement flat stairwells every time he heard voices. It was in one of these that he was skulking now. At least he'd found Naughton Road without too much trouble. He flexed his muscles to assess the damage he'd incurred so far. Several of the blows to his body had been centred on his ribs. Some must have been broken. Bones always took longer to heal than flesh. He preferred to sleep at times like this, to aid the healing process. But he didn't have time for that right now.

He could smell food again. Meat. The smell was all-encompassing and agonizing. He was worried that if he didn't feed soon, he might collapse. It was at times like these that he wondered if he should eat those he killed, but the thought of consuming human flesh inspired nothing but repulsion in him. His strength was already waning. There had been times in the forest when he'd been so hungry he'd blacked out for hours. He couldn't allow that to happen here, not out in the open where anyone could find him. He had to get indoors. Then he could find something to eat. Food, like sleep, would help him heal. The more the better. First he would deal with Mason, then he would gorge himself.

Moving forward out of the shadows, he looked around, and as luck would have it, his eyes fell almost immediately on the door of number eleven. This was it. Mason couldn't elude him any longer. His scent, coupled with the stench of Devoida, was now filling his nostrils. He had him. There was a light on in the window, and . . . Wasn't that someone peeking out into the street? It was. The curtains moved and the face disappeared – but it had been there.

He moved across the road fast, finding the front steps and almost leaping up them in his desire to finish what he'd started. He could smell others now. Perhaps Mason had a family after all. If so, things could get decidedly messy. But if Mason had to watch his family die in front of him, he would only have himself to blame. Haller could hear the curtains in the window rustling: the sound of the material was like sandpaper to his trained ears. He tried shaking his head to remove the dizziness of hunger that was plaguing him, then raised one fist, ready to pound on the door.

Inside the ground-floor flat, Rose Baker turned away from the window to ask her parents what the man downstairs did for a living.

'Don't know,' Mr Baker replied. 'Keeps himself to himself.'

'Maybe he's a policeman,' his daughter suggested.

'Come away from the curtains and stop being so nosy,' her mother said, trying to concentrate on knitting and watch television at the same time.

'Nosy Rosie,' her father added, smiling, his face buried in the newspaper. He looked up, his brow wrinkling. 'What makes you think he might be a policeman?'

'Because I saw a gun when his coat moved.'

Her parents exchanged glances, then got up and moved to the window, pulling the curtains apart to get their own share of the view.

'Where is he?' Her mother craned her neck to see down the street.

'He's gone,' Rose replied, moving away. Suddenly there were three loud knocks on the door.

'Is that him?' There was a nervousness in Mrs Baker's voice.

'No,' Rose replied, shaking her head. 'He went away down the street, towards the main road.'

'Then who's that?' her father asked, trying to see who

was standing outside by the front door, but knowing it was impossible from that angle.

'I'll go and see,' Rose said.

They had almost reached the corner of the road when Gerontius heard Leah take a sharp breath. He looked across at her and saw that she had stopped and was staring back up the pavement, rain running down her cheeks.

'What is it?'

'Come on, guys,' Mason urged. 'We have to keep moving.'

'I saw it,' she answered. 'I saw it by the flat.' Her eyes were wide open.

'Oh Christ,' Mason said. He took her by the arm and pulled her towards the corner. Gerontius followed. They said nothing more as they ran. There wasn't a lot to say.

As the young girl opened the door, her eyes widened in shock, and her lower jaw seemed to hang down.

'Let me in . . .' Haller whispered, his mouth dripping, his throat dry. He stood there, a monstrosity in the rain, his long tongue hanging from one side of his jaw, his shoulders rising and falling with painful, ragged breaths.

'Who is it?' came her mother's voice from the living room.

'Oh no . . .' the girl whispered, unable to tear her gaze from the huge, blood-soaked demon before her. She couldn't move, much less slam the door closed.

'Let me in,' the wolf repeated as he pushed one foot between the door and the frame, the security chain already stretched to its limit. There was a loud scraping noise as the creature dragged its claws down the door, gouging deep trails in it.

'No . . .' The girl was nearly hysterical now. 'No, I won't.'

'Then I'll—'

'Who is it?' Mr Baker called from the living room. His concern was unmistakable. Any further delay and he would come to the hall to see what was going on. Finally able to free herself from her terror-induced paralysis, Rose ran into the living room screaming, and hid behind her father.

'What on earth's the matter, girl? Who's there?' Mr Baker pulled her grasping hands from his jumper and walked over to the living-room door. There were a few seconds of silence, then, as he was about to find out who the strange visitor was, the front door exploded inwards and crashed to the floor. Baker recoiled in shock and staggered backwards into the living room. 'What the—?'

The beast walked in, glaring first at him, then at his wife, then at their daughter. Baker was certain right there and then that he was going to be eaten. He had the urge to laugh, but had no idea why.

'Where is he?' the creature asked.

'Who?' Baker stammered, trying to process what he was seeing.

The creature growled and lunged towards him, grabbing him by the neck and hoisting him into the air. 'Tell me now or I'll bite the girl's head off!'

'Who? Where's who?' Baker gargled, grabbing the creature's arms in an attempt to support his own weight.

'Mason!' Haller squeezed the man's neck harder. If he wasn't careful he'd crush the man's windpipe.

The man groaned for a few moments, then gasped, 'Downstairs! I think Mason is the man who lives downstairs.'

'But this is number eleven,' Haller insisted.

'Yes, yes it is,' Mrs Baker said through her tears, appalled by what was happening to her husband. 'It's eleven A. Downstairs is eleven B.' She stared at the creature's face, trembling in fear. 'Please. Please let my husband go.'

'Urgh!' Haller let go of the man's throat, allowing him to fall to the floor in a heap. He turned to walk out, then stopped and sniffed the air. 'What meat do you have?'

'What?' Mrs Baker rushed over to her husband, who was vigorously rubbing his neck. 'What do you mean?'

'I smell meat! Where is it?'

'The fridge,' Rose said. 'It's in the fridge.'

'Go and get it, girl,' Haller ordered, remaining by the living-room door.

'It's just yesterday's roast,' Mrs Baker said apologetically. 'There's still a lot left on it though. Please don't eat us . . . Oh God.' She started crying again. 'Don't eat us, I beg you!'

Haller wrinkled his snout in disgust. 'I've no intention—'

Rose came back into the room and walked slowly up to Haller, offering the roast up to him like a sacrifice. He grabbed the chicken from the plate, stuffing as much as he could into his jaws. The family winced as they heard the bones cracking and saw the juices dripping from his muzzle. When he'd finished chewing, he muttered something inaudible, then left them and walked down the steps to the flat below. Seconds later they heard another door being destroyed. Mr Baker, still unable to speak, gathered his wife and daughter to him and took them into the bathroom, which had a lock on the door. They sat on the floor next to the bath.

'Shouldn't we ring the police?' Mrs Baker asked.

Her husband and daughter responded with strange looks.

'What are we going to tell them, Mum?'

The door to the basement flat was locked, which was good, because Haller wanted to kick it down. Lurching inside, he sniffed this way and that, desperate now to get his hands on the man who had evaded him at every step. He was here. He must be here, he could smell him. In one swift motion he lifted the coffee table up with one foot and launched it against the wall, where it shattered.

'Come on out, Mason!' he roared. 'Let's finish this now!'

He walked into the kitchen. Nothing. He tried the bathroom. Still nothing. The bedroom . . . Mason had definitely been in here recently. Haller stooped and looked under the bed. No one there. There was no one in the wardrobe either. Where was he hiding? As he was about to close the wardrobe door, he noticed a large metal case lying at the bottom, underneath the hanging clothes. He crouched and opened it. Inside was a large section of grey foam with a number of shapes cut out of it . . . Guns were usually kept in this case, but they weren't here now. He sniffed the handle. It was pungent with gun oil, perspiration, scent. Mason's scent.

He'd taken the guns recently. Not that they'd do him any good.

'Mason!' Haller called out. 'Give yourself up! You can't hide from me!' He tried the bathroom again, checking the cavity underneath the bath in case Mason was hiding there. 'The sooner you give it up, the better. If I have to waste any more time tracking you down, I won't give you an easy death . . .'

He was back in the kitchen now. He checked the small cupboard under the sink. He was beginning to feel like an idiot. He flung the plates and bowls from the draining board, smashing them on the floor. 'Where are you?' Suddenly he caught another scent . . . It was the chemical smell again. It was already a part of Mason's smell, but this was the other one, the one he'd picked up in the theatre. Someone *had* been with Mason, and probably still was. And if that wasn't confusing enough, there was now a third scent. He sniffed around the kitchen units. It was a pleasant, light perfume. A female. What was going on? Had Mason acquired help?

18: WAITING

They didn't stop running. As soon as they were on Bramley Road, they heard the sound of kids playing football at the sports centre, and cars travelling across the busy overpass. As they passed underneath, Gerontius saw a mini-market and an Indian takeaway. An old man standing outside the mini-market waved to Mason in recognition, but there was no time to return the gesture. Every second counted now. It was a question of survival.

Haller walked back into the living room, trying to calm himself so he could think. Mason had come back and taken the guns from the wardrobe. Then he'd left, it seemed, with two others. He wasn't stupid. He knew he didn't have time to hang around. But where would he go? Haller walked over to the doorway and looked up past the railings towards the night sky. *Where are you, Mason? Somewhere you think I won't find you . . . Somewhere I won't be able to touch you? Somewhere with a lot of people? Somewhere out in the open that would be busy all night?* London was full of such places. Haller might have to try all of them, unless he could narrow it down. Looking down, something caught his eye. It was a map that had been blown into a corner near a flowerpot opposite the bottom of the steps. Haller picked it up. On the reverse was a diagram of the underground. Two stations had been ringed. He took a long sniff of the ink and knew that it was fresh, very fresh. Mason, the fool, had left him a burning clue. He then used the map to find the nearest tube station, which was Latimer Road. That must be where Mason was heading now.

His stomach gurgled as it broke down the chicken, bones and all. He felt a little strength returning but his muscles still ached. If only he had time to rest. He left the flat and walked back up the steps to street level. He sniffed but couldn't detect anything helpful. The rain and wind would have removed any scent trails by now anyway. He cursed. He was about to set off when he heard laughter somewhere further down the road. Ducking back down the steps, he hid in the shadows. He couldn't stay here long. The family upstairs might have called the police – or, even worse, the media.

While he waited for the people to pass by, he considered his best course of action. The first thing he had to do was change back into human form. It was too risky going all the way into the centre of town in his current state: the chances of being spotted would increase dramatically, and even if he could keep dodging out of sight, the hunt for Mason would take far too long. And travelling the underground in this guise was also out. So he had no choice but to change back. His face pulled back into itself, while his arms and legs buckled and shrank. When the process had finished, he felt drained. He brushed the discarded teeth and hair from his clothes, then rolled his head around. To add to his discomfort, the calf muscle in his right leg went once more into spasm, along with a muscle in his neck. He gritted his teeth, straightened his leg and rode the wave of agony. Two people passed him on the road above. He lay there, looking like a tramp and feeling like he'd been beaten up. He buttoned his ruined shirt as best he could, but it still looked terrible. Then he remembered something he'd seen in Mason's cupboard; something that could prove very useful. *What the hell*, he thought. *A few more minutes won't make any difference.*

He went back into the flat and opened Mason's wardrobe. He took the bullet-proof vest he'd seen earlier, and also a red silk shirt, black trousers and long black coat. The clothes fitted him well, which was good, except it meant that if he ended up having to transform again, they'd be torn apart. At the bottom of the wardrobe, next to the gun case, were a few pairs of shoes. He took off his shoes, found a pair of socks from a chest of drawers on the other side of the room, then tried on a pair of polished black slip-ons. If it really became necessary to transform again, he'd just have to take them off, but right now his feet were cold.

He left the flat and climbed the steps. As he emerged onto the road, he heard a voice cry out, 'Hey! Hey! Did you see it?' It was an old man who was standing outside one of the houses opposite. 'Did you see the monster?'

Haller turned and smiled at the man. 'Monster?'

'Yes,' the pensioner said, not realizing who he was talking to. 'A w-werewolf!'

Haller's expression remained fixed for a few seconds, then he burst out laughing. 'A werewolf? Don't be ridiculous!' He turned and walked up the road, ignoring the old man's protests.

The station entrance was small, the ticket office unmanned. Mason went straight over to the touch-screen ticket machine and bought three one-day travel cards. He handed over two of them to Gerontius and Leah, and they rushed through the automatic barrier, then round a corner and up a flight of steps to the platform.

'Are we going to Trafalgar Square then?' Leah asked as they clomped noisily up the stairs, pushing past a couple of people who were on their way down. She sounded unsure, perhaps worried that they were making a mistake.

'Yeah,' Mason replied. 'We should be all right there. Hopefully there'll be people around all night.' As they emerged onto the westbound platform, he looked back. Haller surely couldn't be more than a few minutes behind. And if he'd guessed where they'd gone, he would no doubt change back into human form to blend in. Mason had no idea what Haller looked like as a man. All he'd have to go on was his bullet-torn, blood-soaked clothes.

A dishevelled man with a bandage over his eye was sitting on a bench on the opposite platform, singing a Carpenters song. The three of them looked across at him. *What a way to live*, Gerontius thought. *Must be so lonely.*

'Heads up, guys,' Mason said, interrupting the boy's thoughts. 'There's a train coming.'

Once inside the carriage, they squeezed themselves between the other commuters. There was an agonizing wait for the train to set off, but thankfully it pulled away without incident, and they were soon heading towards Hammersmith.

Haller had passed Latimer Road station on his way to Mason's flat. He walked down Naughton Road at a brisk pace, then turned left at the end, so that he emerged onto Bramley Road. He broke into a steady run and nearly collided with a man standing outside the station. Despite the rain, the man had been leaning against a railing, smoking a cigarette. As Haller turned into the entrance, he caught the man giving him a sneer. He ignored it. On another day the stranger might not have been so lucky.

He stood inside the station wondering if Mason had been there only moments before, and if he'd have been able to smell him if he'd still been in wolf form. There was no point in agonizing over it. The game had changed, the rules were different now, so he'd have to get used to them. He passed through the barrier and walked up the two flights of steps to the platform, trying to formulate a plan in his mind. He had to have a firm idea of how he was going to approach Mason, and what he was going to do if the man really did have company. Killing him in public would be tricky enough, without adding two more bodies. He looked around carefully at the people on both platforms, just in case Mason was still there, but he wasn't. He must have caught a train already.

On the platform a voice announced that the next train

wouldn't be along for another four minutes. Haller strolled along the walkway, still thinking, still formulating his plan of action. By the time the approaching roar of the train could be heard, he still hadn't come up with anything. He boarded the train, realizing he'd have to play it by ear. Finding a spot to stand, he held onto the yellow rail and accidentally nudged the back of a younger man standing next to him.

'Hey, watch yourself, mate,' the other passenger snorted.

Haller turned to him and momentarily changed his eyes from brown to shining yellow. The other man's expression faltered, and he turned away quickly. Haller smiled.

The Bakers waited patiently for the police. They knew they might be laughed at, or accused of wasting police time, but their safety was more important than anything. They'd eventually left the bathroom, and emerged into the now cold living room. While Mrs Baker used the phone, her husband crept cautiously to the front door and peered out. The monster seemed to have gone, but how to be sure? He looked at the front door, now lying on the floor of the hall. He took hold of it and managed to manoeuvre it towards the splintered frame. It wouldn't be a perfect fit, but at least it would keep out some of the cold. Before they went to bed, he'd find some way of barricading it, just in case any more unwanted guests turned up.

Mrs Baker had told the police that a wild animal had somehow found its way inside the house, but avoided being specific about the description.

'It was big and vicious,' she said. 'With long hair. It bashed the door right off its hinges. Please come as soon as you can.'

When Evans and Gould arrived, Mr Baker removed the door, showed them in, then put the door back. Gould was already making notes.

'Good evening – you must be Mr Baker,' Evans said.

'Yes, that's right. Please, come in.' He ushered them into the living room, where his wife and daughter were sitting together on the sofa. The television was on, but the sound had been turned right down. They both looked up as the woman and her partner walked in.

'I'm Janice Evans, and this is my colleague Mark Gould. We're from the Metropolitan Police.' This wasn't completely true, but Evans was fast learning that the truth just caused confusion. 'We were told there was a wild animal here. Is that right?'

'Yes, yes, that's right,' Mrs Baker said. 'Please, sit down.' She indicated the free armchair.

'I'll take a look at the door – if that's OK?' Gould turned and walked back out into the hall before anyone could reply.

Mr Baker, unsure what to do for a moment, went towards the kitchen. 'Can I get you and your colleague a cup of tea?'

'Oh, no thank you. We're fine.'

'Oh.' He stopped, then walked over and stood near the hall where he could watch the man examining the front door and hear the conversation in the living room at the same time.

'So,' Evans began, 'what exactly happened?'

'Well . . .' Mrs Baker shifted uncomfortably. 'There was a knock on the door—'

'A knock?'

'Three knocks,' Rose interrupted.

'Like . . . a person knocking?'

'Yes, it sounded a bit like that,' Mrs Baker replied, shaking. 'I think it was trying to break its way in . . . Rosie went to the door to see—'

'And where were you and your husband?'

'Oh, we were by the window.'

'The window?'

'Yes, Rose had been looking out into the street.'

'The man downstairs,' Rose said.

'Yes, she'd just seen the man downstairs leave, and that's when we heard the knocks—'

'I think he's a policeman.'

'Don't interrupt, Rosie,' Mrs Baker said. 'It's rude!'

'Sorry, did you say a policeman?'

'Yes,' Rose replied. 'He had a gun.'

'Rose!' It was her father this time. 'You don't know he was carrying a gun.'

Evans turned to see if her partner had heard all this, but he was obviously busy with the door.

'And what is the gentleman's name? The one who lives downstairs?'

'I think it's Mason,' Mr Baker replied. 'I don't know what his first name is.'

'But he wasn't the one who broke in here, was he? When

you made the emergency call, you stated it was a wild animal.'

'Yes,' Mrs Baker replied. 'Only . . . You see . . .'

'Please – it's OK. You can tell me exactly what happened. I'm very open-minded.'

'Oh,' Mrs Baker replied.

'Could you describe it?'

'Well, it was about seven feet tall, with a muzzle like a dog and – this must sound so silly!'

'It was a werewolf,' Rose blurted. 'That's what it was.'

'OK,' Evans said. 'That's a good start.'

'What – you believe that?' Mr Baker was incredulous.

'Yes, I do,' Evans said, turning to look at him. 'It struck at a mini-market earlier. Luckily no one was hurt, but it's a very dangerous creature and we're very anxious to apprehend it. Now what exactly did it do and say?'

'Well' – Mrs Baker looked at her husband, who closed his eyes and nodded – 'it threatened us, demanded to know where Mr Mason was. And I think Rose saw Mr Mason go down the road towards the station a few minutes before the . . . before we heard it at the door.'

'Yeah, with his kids,' Rose added.

'What? He doesn't have kids, Rosie,' her dad said.

'But there were two with him. A boy and a girl.'

'Jan,' came Gould's voice from the hall, 'I think you'd better come and see this.'

Mr Baker was worried. What could the police do even if they did believe the story? What could anyone do if that thing came back? Turning his head to look into the hall, he watched the policeman crouch over the door, which he'd laid down flat.

'Excuse me,' Evans said as she pushed past Baker. 'What's up?'

'Look at these marks,' Gould said, pushing a lock of hair from his eyes and pointing to one of the door's front panels. He opened the case he'd carried in with him and assembled a large digital camera.

'Yep,' Evans said. 'It's definitely the werewolf.'

19: CIRCUS

They reached Hammersmith station, walked down the platform with its countless movie posters and snack machines, crossed over the busy road and entered the shopping centre to get to the Piccadilly Line. It took only a few minutes to find the right platform and board a train. They said few words to each other on the way, but they all felt their anxiety lift a little. Being amongst large numbers of people gave them the security they needed. Surely, even if the monster did track them down, it couldn't touch them once they were out in the open?

Gerontius was glad to sit down for a few minutes. The day's ordeal had exhausted him, and even though he wouldn't be able to sleep properly, the thought of closing his eyes and slipping away from it all was a welcome one. He glanced at Mason, who kept looking up and down the carriage, as though paranoid that the beast might already be on the train. Mason had risked a lot to keep him safe in the theatre. And now he was taking further risks in order to protect the three of them. Why was he doing it? He didn't stand to gain anything by helping them. Gerontius hadn't seen or heard that much of Cain and Bale, but he'd had the impression that they wouldn't have been as helpful as Mason. So what made him different?

The man in question was finding it very hard to sit still. It was the guns he was carrying. There was already one person sitting to his left, and as they stopped at Earls Court, the seat to the right of him was filled. If he made a wrong move, one or more of the weapons under his coat might poke someone, and then there could be trouble. He looked along the carriage in both directions. There was no one whom he would consider 'suspicious'. Certainly no one with blood all over him. More people boarded the train at Gloucester Road, and by the time they reached Piccadilly Circus the compartment was heaving.

Mason was ready to move, and he made sure his companions were too. They pushed their way through the other commuters and stepped onto the platform. It was evening now, and as he'd hoped, there were a lot of people about. They followed the crowd, heading towards the exit. When they reached the bottom of the long escalator, they saw a busker playing a fiddle. He smiled at them to begin with, then, noticing something under Mason's coat, his bow slipped and made a horrible screeching sound. Mason looked down and saw that his coat was billowing open every now and again, revealing one of his weapons.

'Shit!' He buttoned the coat up and walked on briskly, glad that the startled fiddler had resumed playing behind him.

Minutes later they were climbing the steps out of the station and into the evening air. People pushed past them, there were voices everywhere. Opposite them were the huge bright advertisements for Coke, TDK and Sanyo. Only a few metres away the statue of Eros was gathering its usual crowd of photographers. It was dark, but the neon lights and video displays illuminated a hive of activity. Gerontius watched a group of tourists manically photographing the panorama as their tour bus passed slowly by.

'OK, guys,' Mason said. 'We should probably get away from the station. I think Trafalgar Square might be best, but why don't we get something to eat here first?'

'I'm not really hungry,' Leah said, looking at the people passing by.

'Well, why don't I get you a sandwich or something and if you change your mind . . . you know.'

'OK.' Leah nodded in reply.

'I'm quite hungry now,' Gerontius said.

'Good,' Mason said. 'Me too. There's a café I go to near here. It's a good place.'

They walked away from the station exit. Now, at last, they were beginning to lose themselves.

Crossing the busy road took some time. There were plenty of people about, which was good, when they weren't getting in the way. They walked for a few minutes down the side street that ran parallel to Regent Street. Opposite them, at the junction of two other streets, was the Soup Stone Café.

'Doesn't look very big,' Leah said.

'That's what I like about it, my young friend,' Mason replied. 'You're close to the windows. You can always see what's coming.'

They crossed the road and went in.

*　　*　　*

Ten minutes later an increasingly impatient Haller emerged from Piccadilly Circus station. He gazed around at the multitude of bodies all milling about, crossing the road and going in and out of shops that would be open late into the night. Where would Mason have gone from here? Oxford Street? St James's Park? Or would he have gone straight to the other location ringed on the map? Haller walked over to the Eros statue, where he had a better view of the roads that led off in all directions. Mason would go somewhere busy, but open. That way he would have the protection of the crowd, but be able to see a good distance in all directions. Piccadilly Circus was a good choice, but the number of roads and corners here made it a tricky location to handle. No ... He moved a few metres away from the statue and stopped. In his mind a picture formed of Nelson's Column, illuminated in the darkness. Trafalgar Square. It was the obvious choice. Without further hesitation, he began walking briskly down towards the square, keeping his eyes open for any sign of his quarry.

The Soup Stone was small but busy. There were a couple of tables and chairs outside, which were occupied, despite the cold wind and persistent drizzle. But inside it was warm and Mason found a table near one window with enough room for the three of them to squeeze round. A waitress came over and cleared the table as they sat down. Leah remained dismissive when it came to ordering the food, but Gerontius ordered a burger and Coke for himself and a toasted sandwich and orange juice for her in case she changed her mind. An elderly gentleman was seated directly behind Mason, making him wary of talking about their situation in any detail. Shortly after the food arrived, however, the man left, giving them a degree of privacy.

Gerontius devoured his burger, amazed at how quickly his appetite had returned since leaving Mason's flat. Leah poked at her toasted sandwich with her fork, as though trying to wake it up.

'Are we going to be in the square all night?' she asked.

'Well . . .' Mason tried to finish his mouthful of salad quickly so that he could answer. 'Yeah, I think so. By morning I hope I'll have had some time to think of a more long-term plan.'

'I was thinking,' Leah said. 'Maybe tomorrow – or even before, if it's OK . . .' She paused, deliberately avoiding her cousin's questioning eyes. 'Perhaps you could take us to Mandy's.'

Gerontius, about to take another bite of burger, shook his head.

'Mandy's?' Mason asked. 'Is that a restaurant or something?'

'No,' Gerontius replied. 'It's her friend's house.'

'Oh, I see. Well,' he said, wiping his chin with a napkin, 'I'm not sure that would be a good—'

'At least until my mum and dad get back on Friday.'

'We don't want anyone else involved,' Gerontius insisted, in the middle of chewing another mouthful.

'Look,' Mason said patiently, putting his fork down, 'I know this isn't easy for you guys.' He gave Leah a sympathetic smile. 'But you have to trust me here, OK? I can and will protect you, because I know what's after us – there is no way I'm letting him get his hands on you . . . Understand?' They nodded. 'I've had to react pretty fast today, because he's been right behind me all the time. Once the night's over it'll be harder for him to do anything and not be seen. And like I say, by the morning I should have thought up a better plan. A way of getting you two out of the equation.' They ate in silence for a minute or two. 'By the time your folks get back, this should all be over.'

'What'll happen to you?' Leah asked, appreciating that the man was only trying to help them.

'Don't worry about me,' Mason replied. 'I'll be fine.'

Gerontius looked up at him, not entirely believing what he'd just said.

When they'd finished the meal, Mason paid and they left, finding the rain had returned with a vengeance. They walked back up to Piccadilly Circus, dodging from doorway to doorway until the rain had stopped. Once there, Leah seemed to cheer up a little.

'Can we check out the Virgin Megastore while we're here?'

'Oh, I don't know,' Mason said. 'Well, I guess so . . . It should be pretty safe.'

'Come on,' she said, rushing across the road.

'Is this a good idea?' Gerontius asked. 'Shouldn't we be getting to the square?'

'It might help,' Mason replied. 'I think we could do with a distraction.'

Inside the large building, Leah ran over to the albums

section to look for her favourite artists. Gerontius, keeping an eye on her, chose to take a quick look through the rock albums. Mason stood nearby, alternating his attention from the door to Leah. At one point he happened to glance at the CD Gerontius was examining.

'CCR, eh?'

'Yeah.'

'Good choice.'

'They were one of my dad's favourites. He used to play them all the time.'

'You must miss him bad. Especially now.'

'Yeah, Mum and Dad were the best. When we got back from Austria, Dad was going to teach me to play the guitar. He was going to teach Mum the piano as well.'

'He played the piano too?'

'Yeah.'

'Wow. Talented guy.' Mason smiled.

Gerontius returned the CD to the rack, then reached inside a pocket of his jacket and pulled out his faded leather wallet. In dark lettering on the front, Mason could just make out the word *Vienna*. The boy flicked through some scraps of paper, then pulled out a small photograph. It had been trimmed so that it would fit into the wallet. He showed it to Mason.

'This is them? Good-looking couple.'

'I took it when we were in Austria, not long before . . .'

'They look like great people, Gerry. Really. I'll bet they were very proud of you.'

Gerontius didn't reply; he just replaced the photo,

fighting the tears that were threatening to well up in his eyes again. Just then Leah came bounding over.

'Find anything you like?' Mason asked.

'They don't even have a country/acid/house section . . . Can you believe it?'

'Oh well,' Gerontius said, forgetting the sombre moment.

'Shall we head off then?'

They left the shop and turned in the direction of Lower Regent Street, which would lead them to Pall Mall, and on to Trafalgar Square. The whole world felt different to Gerontius now. He had a strong feeling that something eventful was going to happen, for better or for worse.

20: SQUARE

When Evans and Gould had finished taking the Bakers' statements, they left them to their considerable confusion and went down the steps outside to the basement flat. They hadn't told the Bakers any more than they needed to know, but there was no point in trying to fob them off with a scientific explanation, because there wasn't one. It was a wulver, a lycanthrope – a Lon Chaney Jr, as her first partner had called it, after an actor in an old horror movie. Evans had given the family a phone number for a post-traumatic stress counsellor who worked with the department, and advised them to talk only to him about the incident and no one else. Telling family and friends about it wouldn't do them any good. Only those who had seen the creature with their own eyes would believe it.

They would have knocked on the door of the downstairs flat if it had been attached to its frame. Rain had already soaked a portion of the carpet by the door, so the intruder had clearly been gone a while. Nevertheless, Evans reached into her coat and took out her gun.

'What the hell's that?' Gould asked, surprised to see the weapon.

'Protection.'

'Jesus, we're not authorized to carry guns.'

'No, we're not,' Evans replied firmly. 'Technically we're not authorized to chase after monsters either – but we do it. And I don't intend to do it a second longer without some means of defending myself. Now keep your voice down – it might still be here.' She led the way into the living room.

'It's because of what happened to Talbot, isn't it?'

'What?'

'You weren't carrying a gun then, were you?'

'No . . . I must have been crazy.' Evans moved into the kitchen, turning on the light and scouring the work surfaces for evidence of some kind. As luck would have it, she saw something. Moving forward and replacing her gun, she picked up the long grey hair and held it up so Gould could see. 'This could be it.'

'How can we know for sure?'

'I'll call the office and get them to send a crime scene guy down here immediately. If we can jump to the front of the queue we could get the DNA processed in a couple of hours, maybe sooner. Check the bedroom.'

'What am I looking for?' Gould asked as he opened the wardrobe door.

'Something interesting.'

'Interesting?'

'Yeah, anything that might tell us why our hairy friend was so keen on finding this Mason character.' She left the kitchen and tried the bathroom.

Gould found the case at the bottom of the wardrobe and looked inside. 'Jan,' he called out.

'Yeah?'

'Take a look,' he said, lifting out the case and putting it on the bed where they could both see it better.

Evans came in. 'What is it?'

'Something interesting,' he replied.

Haller walked twice around the square, keeping to the shadows as best he could, but finding it difficult. The area was very exposed and there were more people here than he'd anticipated. But there was no sign of Mason. He stopped by the fountain and took another good look round. Mason had been well ahead of him, so if he was heading for the square, he should have been here by now. So where was he? Could he have been hiding somewhere near his flat, waiting for Haller to leave? He felt the anger boiling inside him again. His destructive desire craved release, filling his head with images of tearing Mason to pieces. He swore and sat down on the edge of the fountain, watching a group of tourists take photographs of each other. If Mason had truly escaped him, the job wasn't complete and Slaughter wouldn't give him the money. What if he just gave up and let his target go? Mason must have realized that Slaughter had ordered him and the others dead because of the job they'd botched. There was a chance he would try and take Slaughter out. If he did, Haller would lose the money, but at least he wouldn't have Slaughter breathing down his neck. No, there were no guarantees . . . And besides, he'd never be able to relax knowing that Mason was out there some-where, silently taunting him. He had to kill him, even if it meant devoting every hour of every day to tracking him down.

He took another walk around the square, then decided to head back up to Piccadilly Circus, in case Mason had turned up there. He walked slowly up Pall Mall, then Lower Regent Street, checking the faces of everyone he passed. And then, just as he was beginning to lose hope entirely, he saw him. Mason was walking in his direction but on the other side of the road. Haller kept his head down and stopped by a shop doorway, pretending to look at the gifts in the window. He found Mason's reflection and this time saw the two youths who were walking beside him. *Who the hell are they?* Haller thought, unable to resist turning round now to look across the street at the trio, who were moving away from him towards the large memorial at the bottom of the hill. *Are they Mason's kids?* he wondered. *He must be mad to endanger them like this. Does he really think I'll leave him alone if his kids are with him?* He couldn't see their faces, but he guessed they were both around fifteen or sixteen years old. Mason was taking a foolish risk. If the kids got in Haller's way, they'd get hurt, and it would be on Mason's head, not his.

They were nearly at the square. So far so good. Mason hadn't seen anyone with torn clothes or blood all over them yet. Perhaps they would be all right after all. They emerged onto Pall Mall, from where they could already see the National Gallery standing proudly at the top of the square. They hurried on, stopping only to allow traffic to pass, and soon entered the square itself. Leah gazed around her, taking in sights she'd seen many times before. Nelson's Column seemed bigger in the dark, watching over the square and its many visitors. They walked past the gallery, then down to the right and around the square, passing one fountain, then the column itself with its proud lions. It was going to be a long night.

'Are you sure we're safer outside than in?' Leah asked, not bothering to turn round.

'Yeah, I reckon so,' Mason answered, with more confidence than he felt. There were a lot of dark places Haller could spring from. Too many. Mason was beginning to confront the truth that had been pushed aside for the last hour or so: he wanted to be outside because he was scared. Being trapped in the theatre with that thing had been more than just claustrophobic. He'd never felt boxed in like that before. 'We have more escape routes out here – less chance of being forced into a corner. Makes sense.'

'Looks busy enough,' Leah said.

'Yeah, I hope so,' Gerontius agreed, shooting a glance at Mason, who returned a look that said: *Don't worry, it's going to be fine.*

Leah walked towards the second fountain and sat on the low wall by the statue of the dolphin and child, reaching her hand into the jet of water that came from the infant's mouth. Gerontius and Mason followed, sitting down on either side of her. She withdrew her hand, shook it, then looked around.

'What if there are more of them?'

'What?' Gerontius turned to her.

'That thing,' she replied, refusing to look him in the eye. 'What if it's not the only one of its kind? What if there are thousands?'

'I think we'd know,' Mason said, scanning their surroundings. 'It'd be hard for them to move about for very long without being noticed. I don't know . . . Maybe there are more, but we shouldn't waste our time worrying about that right now.'

'No,' Gerontius agreed. 'Besides, I think this is the same one that . . . you know . . . in Austria.'

'But how can you be so sure?' Leah turned to him now. 'That was eight years ago.'

'I know but—'

'You two should try and relax,' Mason said. 'I'll keep an eye on things.'

Gerontius couldn't relax. He was starting to shake with worry. He'd heard of people having anxiety attacks, and although he'd never witnessed one, he knew that anyone could have them. There were people everywhere, just as the three of them had counted on. But that made him more, rather than less nervous. Any one of them could be the beast. Mason didn't know what it looked like in human form, and neither did he. It could be sneaking up on them right now.

And indeed, it *was* sneaking up on them. Haller had lingered for a minute or two outside the shop on Lower Regent Street to allow them time to get ahead of him, then he'd ambled slowly back down and along Pall Mall, keeping them in sight until he was once more in the square. All he had to do now was watch and wait for an opportunity. They were sitting on the wall of one of the fountains. Haller wondered what had been going through Mason's mind, and what had possessed him to bring the kids along.

Gerontius glanced at his cousin. He tried to smile reassuringly, but her attention was turned away from him again. She was looking towards the huge steps and the gallery above them. She must be as scared as he was. After all, she'd seen the beast too and could easily have been attacked by it. He'd already lost his parents to that monstrosity: he couldn't bear to lose someone else he cared about. Once more he pondered the bizarre twist of fate that had brought the creature back into his life. Was this somehow meant to happen? Perhaps he had cheated fate eight years ago and forced this situation. He knew he had to focus, to be ready to move at a second's notice, but there were so many questions.

Mason was trying to think like the killer. What would he do if the roles were reversed? It was hard to get a handle on it, but he had to assume the worst, otherwise the beast could end up killing the children as well as himself. He had to stay alert, keep his eyes open. Making a mistake now could prove fatal. He scanned his surroundings again, looking for anyone suspicious, out of place, or just standing still. As his eyes passed over one of the entrances to Charing Cross station far off on the road to his left, they caught something. That coat and the red silk shirt – they were just like the ones he had back at home. Come to think of it, everything the guy was wearing could easily have come from his wardrobe. Maybe he was just being paranoid. But the man was facing in their direction and looking straight at them. *Shit*, Mason thought.

Haller had him. He had him good and proper. But what would Mason do now that he was cornered? There was nowhere he could run where he couldn't be followed. The two kids could complicate things, but . . . *It doesn't really matter*, Haller thought. One way or another, the game was at an end. Mason couldn't win now. He was a dead man.

'That's still open, you know.' It was Leah's voice and it woke both Gerontius and Mason from their thoughts.

'What is?' Gerontius asked.

'The National Gallery,' Leah replied, nodding towards the large building at the top of the square.

'Oh,' Gerontius said. 'So?'

'Well, we could go and have a look. I've never been in there before. And it would help if we kept moving, wouldn't it?' She looked to Mason for confirmation.

'Yeah, I guess so,' Mason said. 'We'd still be safe in there.'

Gerontius looked up at him with a curious expression. He could tell something was up, but before he had a chance to question him, Mason stood and smiled at Leah. 'Come on then, let's go take a look.'

Leah got off the wall and started walking slowly towards the steps without waiting for her cousin. Mason followed.

'Shouldn't we stay out in the open though?' Gerontius asked.

'It'll be fine,' Mason replied, shooting regular glances towards something on the other side of the square. 'There'll be plenty of people in there. More than enough, I should think.' He was panicking, and he hated the feeling. They probably should stay in the square, but he couldn't bear the thought of that thing watching them all the time. He had to get away from its gaze.

'There should be loads of people in there,' Leah said to them, turning and walking backwards to the steps at the top of the square that led up to the gallery. 'It doesn't close until nine. We've got time for a good look round.'

Mason let Gerontius walk past him, then ushered both kids up the steps. When he looked once again in Haller's direction, the man had gone.

21: THE DEATH OF ST SEBASTIAN

As they walked up the steps to the grand building, Mason wondered if they'd made the right decision. Could they lose the beast in there, when it had already found them so quickly? Was it possible to lose the thing at all? Perhaps their best bet now was to keep moving. He'd heard the gallery described as a maze before: that could work to their advantage. But he couldn't escape the fact that his main reason for moving into the gallery was that their pursuer had been watching them. He couldn't stand the thought of it just standing there, staring at the kids.

They turned right at the top of the steps and made for the Getty entrance, where other people seemed to be heading. The main entrance at the top of another flight of steps had been blocked off due to maintenance work. This smaller entrance was reached via a path between the two front lawns, and after passing through the two sets of glass doors, they were inside.

'Wow,' Leah said, impressed, even though it was only a small entrance hall. They climbed a short flight of steps and, looking to their left and right, saw the shop and cafeteria.

'Come on,' Mason said, somewhat hurriedly. 'Let's head

on upstairs. There's an information desk through there. We should get a guidebook or something.'

'Hang on, let's make a donation,' Leah said, looking at the large glass donation box.

'What?'

'It's free, isn't it?' Gerontius asked.

'Yeah,' Leah replied, 'but they ask for a donation. I'm going to give a couple of pounds.' She fished about in her pockets. To her right a woman was having a heated discussion with a gallery official about a poster she wanted to hang up.

'Oh – I didn't bring any money!'

'Never mind,' Mason said. 'Here . . .' He reached into his pocket, pulled out a ten-pound note, folded it and posted it into the collection box. He began to usher Gerontius and Leah towards the information desk. Before he could do so, however, they heard the sound of a scuffle by the entrance. Mason turned and saw Haller struggling with two other men. He pushed Leah and Gerontius towards the information desk and the stairs. They had no time to question his actions and could only guess that their situation had worsened.

Mason kept them moving; as they ran, Leah managed to grab a floor plan from the desk, startling the woman sitting behind it.

'We'll need one of these,' she said. 'Otherwise we'll get lost.'

'Getting lost is what we need right now,' Mason replied. Gerontius wasn't so sure. Mason had gone pale and looked genuinely frightened, more than he had been all day.

'What is it?' Gerontius asked as they climbed the steps towards the first floor. 'Did you see something outside?'

Mason looked down at him. 'Maybe. It could have been nothing though. I guess I'm just a little spooked.'

At the top they turned left and round past the elevator to the grand three-door entrance to the central hall.

Haller was amazed to see the trio still in the foyer of the gallery. He'd expected them to be upstairs, finding the furthest possible room from the entrance, or the one with the most exits. Strange, but he wasn't exactly disappointed. He'd won, after all. Mason was his now. He'd stood outside the glass doors, waiting for Mason to make eye contact. The look on his face! Ha! He couldn't have looked more terrified if he'd tried. As Mason pulled the kids away, Haller had grasped the handle of the door and stepped inside. Just then, as he was going up the stairs, two teenagers ran into him from behind, nearly knocking him over.

'What the hell . . . ?' He'd turned and glared at the closest one, a bearded youth with red, dreadlocked hair who was almost on his knees, hanging onto the handrail.

To Haller's great annoyance the kid was now laughing; he reeked of alcohol.

'Sorry, mate,' the teenager offered, still giggling and grabbing onto his friend, another youth with metal studs in his face.

'Get the fuck out of my way!' Haller roared.

'Calm down,' the kid said, getting to his feet. 'Just having a bit of fun.'

'Have fun somewhere else.' Haller pushed the kid aside with rather too much force, and didn't bother to look back when he heard him cry out in pain. He marched to the top of the steps, ignoring the collection box, and went straight towards the information area.

'Hey,' the gallery official called out. 'Just a minute! This poor young man . . .' The voice trailed off as Haller mounted the staircase at speed, barging past several visitors on the way.

'Are you sure everything's OK?' Gerontius asked.

'What? Yeah, of course.' Mason pretended to be surprised. 'Everything's under control, don't worry.' They entered the large central hall and looked around. Leah's trainers squeaked on the wood floor. It was only now that she realized how many people were around.

'Wow, this place really is popular.'

Besides the three of them there were at least ten other people in that room alone. Leah studied the plan she'd opened out.

'OK, let's see . . . *The Virgin of the Rocks* – that's Leonardo da Vinci . . . And *The Ambassadors* – we could go and look at that, it's supposed to be pretty cool.' She looked at Gerontius, seeing that he, like her, was trying to stay calm.

Mason looked down at the plan. 'All right, let's go,' he said. Just then one of the doors behind them opened and a group of Japanese tourists came in. Mason breathed a sigh of relief. 'Come on.' They went through the door on their left, past a stairwell and into another room.

'This is room twelve,' Leah said, her attention focused on the floor plan. 'We need to go into the next one, then turn left. The room with *The Ambassadors* is the one at the end.'

'Dad brought me here when I was little,' Gerontius said, looking around. 'He was a big fan.' Mason couldn't ignore the note of sadness. 'I can remember *Sunflowers*, and some other Van Gogh paintings – maybe the Constables too . . . It seems like so long ago now though. I haven't been back since the accident because . . . well . . . I didn't really feel like it, you know?'

'Yeah, well, you'll have plenty of opportunities to come back and have a proper look,' Mason said.

'Yeah.'

'Definitely,' Leah agreed. 'We'll make it a regular thing. Keep coming back until we've seen everything.'

'Sure,' Gerontius said.

A few minutes later they found themselves in room four, where a tour guide was talking to a small group of visitors. They approached the group and stood listening. Mason turned round so that he had his back to the painting everyone was looking at. The guard, sitting at the other end of the room, gave him a strange look. Mason realized how odd he must look, staring at the doorway rather than at any of the exhibits, but he couldn't afford to blend in just for the sake of appearances.

'. . . once the war-damage repairs were complete, this

painting was remounted here and given pride of place,' the guide said. 'And quite rightly so.'

'It's *The Ambassadors*,' Leah whispered to the other two.

'Maybe we should try somewhere else now,' Mason said, ignoring the guide's words. 'Keep on the move, you know.'

'As with Dehoozo's painting *The Goddess of Curiosity*, which we saw earlier,' the guide continued, 'this piece incorporates "anamorphosis". If you stand to the right of the picture, you'll see exactly what the unusual blur in the foreground is, as your perspective changes.'

The visitors took turns to stand to one side of the painting, each one nodding as the mystery was revealed. Leah joined the small crowd, curious to see what the object was. Once it had become clear, her expression darkened. It was a skull, and it appeared to be grinning.

'What is it?' Gerontius asked as Leah approached.

'Nothing much,' she said. 'Let's try another room.'

'This way.' Mason led them out through the door to their right, eager to keep moving.

Haller thought he heard the crackle of a radio as he mounted the staircase, but he could have imagined it. He hadn't wanted to draw any unnecessary attention to himself, but it was too late now. At the top of the stairs he walked round and into the central hall. The Japanese tourists were now huddled around a painting of an elegantly dressed gentleman. Haller ignored them and tried the door to his right. He passed quickly through this and the room beyond, then found himself in a round chamber with three more rooms leading off it. He looked in each direction. There were people around, but not the ones he was looking for. An elderly gentleman was standing nearby, so Haller walked over and addressed him.

'Excuse me, I've lost my friends. You haven't seen a tall, well-built man come through here with a boy and a girl, have you?'

'No, I don't think so,' the man replied.

Haller only then saw the guard sitting nearby. The guard shook his head to indicate he hadn't seen them either.

'Hmph,' Haller said, and returned to the central hall, where he took the opposite door and kept going until he'd passed the point where the three had turned left, heading straight on instead, towards the Sainsbury Wing.

Leah wanted to lead the way, and Mason had to keep overtaking her to make sure she wasn't exposed to attack. They moved quickly through rooms seven and eight, then room nine, which Haller had passed through only moments before on his way to the Sainsbury Wing. If Mason had chosen to look to the left instead of right at that point, he would have seen the back of their pursuer disappearing through a door. They continued, entering what Leah, consulting her floor plan, announced was the 'orange bit'. The first rooms in this section were quite small, with few other visitors present, so they walked on, passing another stairwell, then entering room twenty-four, the ABN AMRO room.

'Weird name,' Leah said, looking up at the name of the room in big letters on the far wall. 'There's some

Rembrandts around here somewhere— God, look at that!' She pointed to a painting on the wall to their right, depicting a dragon sinking its teeth into the cheek of a man, while the head of another lay nearby. 'It's horrible.' Her face wrinkled in disgust.

Gerontius had to agree. The painting did seem a little out of place with all the others they'd seen – and quite forbidding too. He turned away from it. Mason, after ensuring he knew where all the exits were, and glancing at Leah's floor plan to get a general overview of the area, shot a glance at the small plaque next to the painting: *Two Followers of Cadmus Devoured by a Dragon*. It was only then that he realized the kids were no longer at his side. They'd walked over to another painting by the door at the far end.

'Hey, you guys, for God's sake don't sneak off!' He walked up and saw the guard smile, as though he'd witnessed this a dozen times.

Mason gave him a smile in return. 'At least they're enthusiastic,' he said. The guard nodded in agreement.

'*Saint Sebastian . . .*' Leah read the rest of the plaque to herself. In the painting, the saint himself lay dead or dying, tied to a tree, with several arrows piercing his flesh.

Gerontius read the plaque too. But Mason had decided they'd spent enough time in the room, and placed his hands on the kids' shoulders. He was about to speak when he heard the most chilling scream.

22: THE GALLERY BEAST

It hadn't taken long for Haller to decide he'd had enough. Every room he'd entered had revealed nothing but a solitary guard and more plodding visitors. He was sick of it. Their staring faces, the effort it took not to glare at all of them, along with the impediment of not having his acute senses to work with. He'd stopped and tried to regulate his breathing, knowing that losing his temper would affect his thinking. If they had been crafty, Mason and the kids might have found their way outside again by now. If only he'd stayed in the square and waited for them. They'd have had to leave at closing time: he could have got to them then.

'There he is!' The voice made him turn round. He recognized the gallery official from the foyer – accompanied by a security guard. The room guard, who'd been sitting in his chair quietly watching Haller, stood up and joined the two men. 'That's the one who hurt the young man,' the official continued. 'Nearly broke his arm!'

The large security guard nodded and walked up to Haller, crossing his arms. Calmly, and with a slight smile, Haller bent down and took off his shoes.

The security guard was perplexed, but continued anyway.

'I've been instructed to ask you to leave, sir,' he said clearly. 'I'm afraid the gallery won't tolerate—'

Haller growled. Softly at first, then rising in volume. The security guard was baffled. Haller growled again, louder this time, the sound inhuman enough to unsettle the two guards and the official. He turned to face them, the yellow blaze in his eyes unmistakable. The security guard backed away clumsily, his lower lip trembling, as hair broke out all over Haller's face.

'Jesus,' the official said, also moving out of the room, and almost stumbling into the room guard, who'd had the sense to move seconds before. The three of them turned and ran as Haller's transformation came into full effect. His clothes – or rather Mason's clothes – stretched and tore in several places, until they hung in loose shreds. He watched the men run away like startled lambs, then turned and headed off in the opposite direction, bounding through a number of rooms before finding himself back on the bridge between the Sainsbury Wing and the rest of the gallery. He stopped halfway across, beside the huge grey pillars, and breathed in a huge lungful of air through his nostrils. *Aaaaah . . . yes . . .*

'Masonnnnn!' He screamed his delight at having the man's scent in his airways once more, and the knowledge that his prey was still inside the gallery. Wasting not a second more, he took huge, swift strides in the direction Mason's scent led him.

His heavy footsteps made loud thudding noises as he headed on through the numerous rooms. In each one a startled guard looked up, saw the monstrous form hurtling towards them and either fainted, threw themselves to the floor, or just shrieked in terror. When Haller found the ABN AMRO room, he had no time to slow down before landing on top of the guard, who'd come to find out what all the screaming was about. They both hurtled to the floor, Haller scrabbling for purchase on the polished surface, finding his claws caught in the guard's jumper. He growled and managed to get to his feet, pulling clumps of material from the guard's uniform in the process.

'You idiot!' he spat. The guard, terrified and already stunned by the appearance of the frightening beast, scrabbled away on the floor towards the other doorway.

Haller seethed at the whimpering guard, thoughts of murder running through his head. Then he noticed the painting on the wall to his right: *Two Followers of Cadmus Devoured by a Dragon*. He stared at the winged beast for a moment, feeling a thrill run through him. The painting must be priceless . . . He raised one paw to the top right-hand corner of the canvas, then turned and glared at the guard. The man was still shifting along the floor on his backside when he understood Haller's intent. He stopped.

'N-no! Wait! Don't do that!' He got to his feet now, albeit shakily.

Haller laughed, and dug his claws into the crusty paint.

'No,' the guard insisted, moving forward, astonishingly, back into the room. 'Please . . .' The man seemed to be crying now.

Haller knew he was wasting time, letting his targets get

away, but this was worth it. In one swift motion, his claws rent the canvas from corner to corner, leaving four deep gouges that passed through the head of the dragon and ended in the shoulder of the man he was devouring. To the guard the sound was like the end of the world. He screamed as Haller ran out of the room, laughing like a demon.

The shock hit all three of them at the same time, as did the urge to run as fast as they could away from the guard's scream. Their pursuer must have changed again, something Mason hadn't counted on. The idea seemed so ludicrous. How could he possibly hope to get away with it? The police, media and anyone with an ounce of curiosity would be descending on the gallery in no time. Was he insane? As they ran out of room twenty-eight and into the long series of rooms that led towards the far end of the gallery, two security guards passed them; one advised them to get down-stairs as fast as they could. Some people were still standing and looking at paintings, ignoring the shouts around them. A couple of violinists in one of the long rooms even con-tinued playing, oblivious to the panic that was beginning to grip the building.

They continued along towards the corner room, Leah trying to read the floor plan as they went.

'At the end we go right,' she said as they ran. 'Then once we're at the front, there should be some stairs going down—'

Just then there was an awesome bellow from somewhere behind them, and the sound of one of the pictures hitting the floor. Leah didn't turn to look, but she screamed all the same.

Haller hurtled into the long row of rooms and immediately saw Mason and the two youngsters in the distance. He bounded forward, straight past two visitors, who didn't turn to look at him, even when he threw one of the smaller paintings from the wall in his rage. He presumed they were either deaf or scared rigid. Gritting his teeth and clenching his fists as he ran, he prepared himself for murder, for absolute destruction. Anyone who got between him and Mason now would be torn to pieces. He knew full well that the police would soon be on their way, but he'd deal with them when he'd finished the job. Just before he'd transformed, something had become clear to him. Mason wouldn't have expected him to change, he'd have expected him to be quiet, cautious. Therefore doing the opposite was the key to success. And although he didn't want people to see him, to raise the alarm, the only way he could kill Mason quickly was to become the beast and utilize all the advantages that it offered. It made perfect sense. He passed a glass display case containing a sculpture, and pushed it over, letting it hit the floor and shatter. He was gaining on them now. There was no way out, nowhere they could run.

They were nearly at the end room – number thirty-three on the floor plan. Screams erupted from the small group of people nearby as they saw what was approaching. Through the glass of one of the doors they saw a female guard gazing at them, a questioning look on her face as she adjusted her glasses.

'Get out of the way!' Mason yelled. 'It's coming!'

At first the woman didn't understand what he was talking about; then, when she'd focused on the monster rushing down the large room behind the trio, leaping over the padded benches, her eyes widened, and she fled through the other doorway, screaming in terror. They flew through the doors into the room, Leah and Gerontius rushing immediately to the open doorway ahead of them. Mason chose that late moment to draw a gun from inside his coat. He turned, stood between the two doors and, before he could aim the gun properly, fired at the beast, hearing the bullet embed itself in something soft beneath the creature's shirt.

The weapon was thrown from his grasp as he was hit with the full force of Haller's sudden, powerful lunge. He fell to the floor, nearly banging his head on the circular bench in the middle of the room. Winded and with bright colours flashing around his vision, he tried to get back on his feet. The pain in his side flared, and he could feel the bleeding resume. He groaned and tried to turn over. As he did so, the beast knelt over him and pinned his arms down. It laughed.

Haller felt so much better now. The situation was resolving itself nicely: he was about to deal the deathblow. He let go of Mason's left arm and quickly punched him in the face, almost knocking him unconscious. He was aware of the shouting and screaming of confused guards and visitors still trying to flee the building. He raised his paw to strike again, but this time raked Mason's chest with his claws. The man screamed, then tried to silence his pain behind gritted teeth.

'Go on,' Haller urged in his gruff voice. 'Let it all out.' Then he opened his muzzle wide, saliva dripping from the bottom jaw, and was about to sink his teeth into the man's face when he saw the two children standing in the doorway to his right. At first he chuckled – the looks on their faces were delightful – but the mirth left him as the boy's face lit a spark of recognition within him. His jaws closed again involuntarily.

This can't be possible . . .

He could barely believe what he was seeing. It had been eight long years, but the boy's features were still recognizable. He couldn't move. It didn't make sense. What was the boy doing here? He sniffed hard. The boy carried the same infuriating smell of Devoida as Mason. Had he been in the theatre? An object was suddenly jammed up inside the bullet-proof vest Haller had taken from Mason's wardrobe. He couldn't tear his gaze from the boy, but he had a horrible feeling that the object was the barrel of a gun. There was a loud noise, a white light, and when his vision cleared he was slumped against one wall of room thirty-three, staring at Mason, who was now rising to his feet. Haller coughed up something that tasted metallic. Blood. Not good.

Mason walked over and pointed the gun at Haller's head. 'How's the old heart? Not too good right now, I'll bet. Why don't I try for the brain this time?'

'I wouldn't do that if I were you.' Haller coughed again.

'Oh yeah, why's that?'

'I don't want them to see,' Haller replied, indicating the other two.

'That's very considerate of you,' Mason said, keeping his eyes on the beast.

'It's all right,' Gerontius said. 'Do it. We're OK.'

'There – you heard him,' Mason said. 'They're tough kids.' His finger tensed on the trigger. 'Besides, you're a monster, not a man.'

'Wait,' Haller insisted urgently. 'There's another reason. Send them away and I'll explain.'

Mason thought quickly. On reflection, letting the children see Haller's death wouldn't do them any good, especially if the beast changed back into a man when it died. 'Go on, guys, head on outside into the square. I'll meet you by the fountain.'

'But he—' Leah began.

'Just go! Now!'

Gerontius and Leah exchanged glances. They didn't want to leave. They'd already formed a bond with the man who'd sworn to protect them, and even though it seemed clear that he was moments away from finishing the monster, they found it hard to walk away with the thing still breathing. Nevertheless, they turned to leave.

'See you outside,' Gerontius said, and they left, their rapid footsteps echoing away down the next room.

Mason actually felt more vulnerable now they had gone. 'OK,' he whispered to the beast. 'We don't have much time, so if you've got something to say, I suggest you say it now.'

'The boy,' Haller said, almost in a gargle as more blood dripped from his jaws. He coughed and spat.

'It was you, wasn't it?' Mason asked. 'You were the one who killed his parents.'

'Well,' Haller said, in considerable pain now. 'It depends on your point of view.'

23: THREES

'Gould,' Evans said, coming into the office holding a brown folder, 'I've got the test results on the hair we found at Mason's place.'

'Wow,' he said. 'That was record time.' He swivelled round in his chair to face her.

'I have friends in all the right places,' she said, tapping the folder with her nails.

Gould waited for the information, confused by the odd expression on his partner's face. 'What? What is it?'

'You know how this case seems to have gone from weird to downright baffling?'

'Yeah . . .'

'Well' – she dropped the folder onto the desk beside him – 'it's been upgraded to insane.'

Gould picked up the folder and opened it, taking the sheets of paper from within.

'The DNA from the hair,' Evans continued, 'matched the DNA taken from a man arrested for assault nine years ago. He was acquitted, but his DNA was kept on file. Anyway, as you can see, there's a problem.'

'This doesn't make sense.' Gould's forehead creased. 'They must have made a mistake.' He looked up at Evans.

'I know how it sounds,' his colleague replied. 'But when you think about it, it kind of adds up.'

Just then Evans's phone rang. She picked it up, just as Gould's rang too. They both made notes, then, when they had finished their calls, looked up at each other expectantly.

'You go first,' Gould said.

'We've got an incident at the National Gallery. A lunatic "behaving like an animal". Though that's probably an understatement going by today's events. What they probably mean is they've got a lycanthrope. Come on, let's go.' They both stood and took their jackets from the coat stand. 'What did you get?'

'Exactly the same,' Gould replied. 'Though the description I was given was of a gorilla-like animal.'

'Well, you never know.'

They left the office and ran down the hall, where a colleague in uniform stopped them.

'Hey, you two! We got a call about a body found in a scrap yard. Looks like it was mauled by an animal.'

'How long ago was this?' Evans asked.

'He's been dead for a few hours.'

'Then it can wait.' They barged through the front doors and out into the street, where the car was parked.

'It all seems to be happening at once,' Gould said, shaking his head. 'First it shows up in the mini-market, and now these two incidents.'

'Yeah,' Evans replied, opening the door and settling into the driver's seat. 'It's the law of threes. Which means the gallery is where it ends.'

'Are you sure the DNA tests are correct?' Gould asked as they made their way to the gallery.

'You saw the results . . . And it all seems to add up, don't you think? Like a big crazy puzzle.'

'But he was buried! Someone must have made a mistake.'

'Yeah,' Evans said, weaving deftly through the busy traffic. 'You're not kidding.'

'All right, you've got three seconds to talk before I kill you,' Mason said. 'One . . . two . . .'

'All right,' Haller said. 'I'm telling you this because that boy mustn't see me, even when I'm dead – you must keep the truth from him.'

'What truth?'

'H-he . . .' Haller choked on his words and had to begin again. 'He made me remember what I once was – when I saw his face just now . . .'

'Yeah? And what were you?'

'A father.'

'So? Is this gonna be some sort of sob story? Because if it is, I don't have time.' The sirens were louder now. Mason was getting seriously impatient.

'I was *his* father.'

'He died eight years ago,' Gould said, holding onto the inside door handle as Evans increased speed. 'His body was retrieved from the crash site. There's a burial record and everything.'

'Yeah, there is,' Evans conceded. 'But the body was never

properly identified. The wounds – which, incidentally, were said to have been caused by an attack from a wild animal – completely disfigured the face. In order to avoid putting the son through any more trauma, his parents' bodies were flown back to the UK and buried almost immediately.'

'Jesus,' Gould said. 'No one checked.'

'Nope. And that's one reason we're in this mess right now. But you want to know what really annoys me?'

'What?'

'I'm beginning to actually sympathize with the bastard.'

'What?'

'I think I can see how it all happened.'

'How?'

'The car goes off the road, right? Possibly as a result of being attacked by another creature. It turns over, the family are pretty shaken up, giving the beast a perfect opportunity to drag them out and kill them. Then, after he's mauled the mother and father, he goes back to the car for the kid. But the father isn't completely dead, and because he's been bitten, he changes.'

'Right . . .'

'Right. Now, as we've discussed before, a man's personality doesn't change when he becomes a wulver. The various physical differences do exert an influence on his behaviour, but his mind isn't altered. So in the case of the car accident, what's the father's first instinct once he's transformed and has surveyed the carnage before him?'

'To protect his family . . . And if they're already dead . . . Revenge?'

'Exactly. He tears the other creature apart in his rage. Maybe the other one isn't expecting it and is caught off guard.'

'Then?'

'Then the father dresses the body of the other one, now human again, in his own clothes – maybe mauls the face a bit more just in case the son is asked to identify it, then . . . disappears. He takes off. Wanders around Austria, living on his wits, keeping out of trouble . . . until now.'

'But what kind of a dad would just abandon his son like that? He can't have cared much, or he'd have come back for him.'

'That's where you're wrong. If he'd found his son, he'd have put him in great danger. He threw away everything he had . . . in order to stop himself from harming him. That's an enormous sacrifice. He must have loved his son dearly to have done that.'

'But he *has* come back,' Gould said, unconvinced by Evans's explanation.

'Yeah, but I don't think he came back for his son. I think the disease took its toll on him. He might have forgotten what kept him away from here in the first place. The disease is a powerful one. It consumes its host, changes him, in more ways than one. Although the personality remains the same, the disease exerts a negative psychological effect.'

'Yeah. I'll bet it does.'

'What . . . ?' The gun in Mason's hand wavered.

'Hard to believe, isn't it?'

'You have got to be kidding.'

'No . . . I'm not.'

'Oh Jesus.' Mason tried to fit what Hans had told him with the death of Gerontius's parents. If the old man had been right, if there had only been three werewolves, and this was the third, then it was the second one that had killed the kid's parents – or rather, had tried to kill them. Had Hans really been hunting the boy's father all this time?

'It's strange,' Haller continued, 'but I'd actually forgotten about him, and my wife, until just now. I . . . Oh God . . . I don't know how he got caught up in this. I had no idea he'd be in that theatre. I didn't know he was with you . . .'

'No, this can't be real. You were the one who killed his parents. You must have been.' Nevertheless, Mason was finding it harder and harder to pull the trigger.

'You've no idea how hard it was to leave him that day. I'd already lost my wife. But I knew what I'd become, and how dangerous I was. I had to stay away from him because of the threat I posed. The decision tore me apart, but I had to do it.'

'Change back,' Mason said.

'What?'

'I've seen a photograph of Gerry's dad. Change back and I'll know if you're telling the truth.'

'Does it matter? I'll be dead soon anyway. You'll have your proof one way or another.'

'Just do it!'

'All right . . .'

There was a pause as Haller concentrated his efforts on

transforming. The bullet had penetrated his heart and it refused to heal. His strength had all but left him. Then, slowly, his body reverted to its human state. The hair on his face and hands fell out. Mason cringed as he watched the sharp teeth fall out, to be replaced by human ones.

It was the longest, most painful transformation ever, and to Haller it was the most significant. When it was over, it felt like every muscle in his body was suffering from acute cramp, but he didn't care any more; the pain had blended into a single numbing sensation. He felt tired. More tired than he'd ever been in his life. He let out a long, laboured breath and looked up at Mason, who'd returned the gun to its holster.

'Well?'

'Yeah, you're him.' The resemblance to the photograph in Gerontius's wallet was unmistakable. 'I've got to get you out of here.'

There were voices now, and the sound of two-way radios, from the long row of rooms. Mason grabbed Haller and hoisted him to his feet. 'You're going to need to help me out a bit,' Mason said.

'I'm weak.'

'Yeah, I know, but if we're caught, the police might lock us both up – I've been up to no good myself recently – and then your face will be all over the newspapers where Gerry can see it.'

'There's a back staircase we can use with a fire exit at the bottom. It's the safest bet.'

'Which direction?'

'Down there,' Haller said, pointing towards the front of the building, away from the voices. 'Trust me, I've been here before.'

Evans parked along the side of the square, ignoring the shouts and beeping from other drivers. Running up to the gallery, she could already see three squad cars, a police van and uniformed officers standing at the Getty entrance, stopping people from going inside. The two officers showed their identity badges at the door and walked in. A gallery official was talking to a plain-clothes officer and a constable. Evans and Gould walked over to the group and introduced themselves. The officer in plain clothes nodded.

'I'm Detective Sergeant Lockhart. I'm glad you guys are here. Perhaps you can make sense out of what these people are saying.' He indicated the official with a nod. 'This is Donald Finney, he's in charge of gallery security. He says a "creature" is running around up there. I asked him what sort of "creature" and he said . . . a man!'

'Yes, but it was a man,' the exasperated official blurted. 'Then it . . . changed.'

'OK,' Evans said. 'Where is it now?'

'Still upstairs,' the official replied. 'It was last seen in room thirty-three. We've kept away until now, but some of the police officers were making their way there.'

'Yeah,' DS Lockhart added. 'Officers and security staff are covering the stairwells too. We think all the visitors and guards have been evacuated now. They're all over by the steps to the square.'

'Good,' Evans said. 'Just to be safe, I want you to call for armed officers.'

'What?' Lockhart wasn't sure he'd heard her correctly to begin with. 'Armed? Are you serious?'

'Yes, I am. Come on,' she said to Gould. 'Let's go up.'

'Hang on,' Lockhart called out after them. 'How do you know this man has a weapon?'

'We don't,' she replied, turning back to him. 'But you'll need armed officers either way.'

Lockhart instructed his constable to call for backup. Evans and Gould carried on towards the stairs.

'Whoa!' Lockhart trotted after them. 'Aren't you going to wait until they get here?'

'We've got protection,' Evans answered. And before Lockhart could voice his objections, she and Gould were on the staircase by the information desk, heading up towards the central hall.

They sat on the steps listening to their own laboured breathing. The only other sound in the stairwell was the occasional hiss of the officer's radio at the bottom. He didn't know they were there, and thankfully there was no sign of him moving from his position. They weren't sure why they hadn't gone straight outside like Mason had told them. Perhaps they didn't feel it was time to say goodbye just yet, or perhaps they wanted to be sure that the beast had been killed.

'Let's go,' Leah whispered, squeezing Gerontius's hand.

'No, he'll be here soon, then we can all go outside together. I'm not leaving him – he saved our lives.'

'But it's safer out there.'

'We're all right where we are.'

'Yeah, sure!' Leah spoke out loud, not meaning to. Immediately she clasped her hand around her mouth.

Gerontius stared at her, then looked down the stairwell. There was movement below. They both considered running, but what would be the point? They'd be caught eventually, and then awkward questions would be asked.

'Who's there?' The voice was authoritative, but sounded nervous.

'We're coming down,' Gerontius said, giving Leah a disapproving look. They moved down the stairs until they could see the uniformed officer.

'What are you kids doing in here? You should be outside.'

'Yeah – we heard shouting and hid on the stairs. Something strange was going on.' Gerontius pretended to be even more scared than he was.

'Come on,' the officer replied. 'This way.'

They didn't hear it, but just then the door closest to where they'd been sitting opened.

On the first floor, Evans and Gould found a security guard, who took them into the long corridor of rooms leading to room thirty-three. They were still a little way along from it, but the guard would go no further.

'Right at the end. That's where it was last seen. My colleague says it attacked a man and two children. I dread to think what you'll find down there.' The guard turned and went back towards the central hall.

Gould had a sick feeling in the pit of his stomach. 'This isn't going to be nice, is it, Jan?'

'No,' she replied, drawing her gun. 'Probably not.'

They advanced through each room slowly, cautiously, listening for anything that might signal danger. When at last they reached room thirty-three, they stopped at the threshold. Evans was shaking, and was glad to see that Gould was trembling too. She took a deep breath and moved into the room. Nothing. She breathed again. On the floor was a pool of blood, then drops and smears of it leading away out of the other door. She moved and looked through the doorway and along the next row of rooms. Where had it gone? And where were the man and children? Had they left the gallery?

Gould appeared by her side.

'Come on,' she said. 'This isn't over yet.'

24: DEADLY ENMITY

Mason had so much trouble trying to get the door open that Haller did it for him. As he did so, Mason noticed how deathly pale the man's hand was. He really was dying.

'There may be someone at the bottom,' Haller said. 'Are you prepared to deal with them?'

'Don't worry,' Mason replied. 'I'll do what I have to.' He helped the bleeding man down the stairs to the ground floor, where he found a large locked door which he presumed led outside. He propped Haller against the wall, then went over to the fire exit. As he cocked the weapon, he heard Haller chuckle.

'What are you laughing at?'

'I just can't believe we're in this situation. You're helping me when you must be dying to kill me.'

'You're dead already. It wouldn't give me any pleasure to finish you off. Where exactly are we supposed to be going anyway?'

'If you can get me out of the city, I'll find somewhere I can die in peace. And where I'll never be found.' Haller groaned with renewed pain.

'What the hell . . . ?' It was a policeman who'd just come through the other doorway.

221

Haller just stared at him, blood soaking his shirt. Mason, thinking more quickly, lunged straight at the constable, striking him a blow across the head and knocking him unconscious.

'Nice one,' Haller said. 'You know, I really don't feel good. We'd better hurry up.'

Mason left the policeman and walked back over to the door. He pushed the bar in hard, and the door opened. Immediately he was hit by a rush of cool air. He supported Haller once more and helped him out of the building. They found themselves to the side of the gallery, only a few paces from the top of the square. They could hear excited chatter and the blaring of more than one siren.

'I'm not sure we're going to get far,' Mason said.

'We can't go down to Charing Cross tube because the police will see us. Best we go up past the Portrait Gallery and head towards Leicester Square.' Haller spat more blood onto the floor.

'OK . . .' Mason took a deep breath. 'Here goes nothing.'

They lurched out into the night, and were immediately faced by an iron railing.

'Shit,' Mason spat. 'Can you see a gate or anything?'

'No – there's no time anyway. You'll have to help me over.'

'Ah, Christ.' Mason stooped and laced his fingers together, giving Haller a foothold.

Haller grabbed the top of the railings, put his right foot in Mason's hands and hoisted himself over, landing hard on the pavement on the other side. He stumbled and nearly lost his balance. Mason had his hands on the top of the railing when Haller suddenly doubled up in pain.

'What's the matter?'

'My body – it's stopped trying to heal . . . It's going the other way now.'

'The other way? What are you talking about?'

'It's . . .' Haller's eyes were wide open, the veins in his forehead bulging. He was in agony. 'I think it's breaking down. Oh God.' He screamed, drawing glances from people nearby.

Mason tried to climb up the railings, but slid back down. Haller screamed again, then turned and ran across the road, transforming painfully as he went, narrowly avoiding a car, before scrambling up the steps of the church of St Martin-in-the-Fields. The strain and discomfort of the change nearly made him pass out.

The few people who had been inside the church soon fled when they saw the monster tear down the central aisle. When Haller reached the end, he collapsed onto his knees beneath the altar. His strength continued to ebb; he wanted to sleep so badly that his eyelids kept falling and then rising again as he fought off unconsciousness. He didn't want to die, but he didn't want the pain to continue either. His perforated heart was struggling with the effort of pumping blood around his body. The curse was still with him, but its healing power had gone. He looked at his paws. Clenching them into fists, he could feel several of his nails give slightly. They hurt too. His tongue rolled around his jaws, testing teeth and finding a number of them loose. *This is it*, he thought. *This is where it ends.*

Bellowing, he slumped to the floor of the church, crashing onto his back, staring up at the ceiling, as blood pooled slowly around his matted fur. New pain exploded all over his body as he deflated back into human form again. He realized with both horror and disgust that his lower jaw had somehow stuck mid-transformation, along with his left leg, which was left throbbing and distended, the veins bulging in several places. As the pain continued to rack his body, he roared and flapped his limbs about in a desperate attempt to complete the change. Was this his final punishment? Is this how he would be found, a malformed freak?

Back behind the railing, Mason could only stare, paralysed at what had happened. What the hell was Haller doing? If he really wanted a quiet end, somewhere out in the wilderness, this wasn't the way to go about it.

'Shit!' Keeping Haller out of the arms of the authorities would now be next to impossible. Just then he heard the fire-escape door open behind him.

'Stay exactly where you are and don't move!'

He didn't.

Finding him hadn't exactly been difficult. They'd just followed the drops of blood. When they reached the bottom of the stairwell, they found the constable slumped awkwardly against a door, his head already swelling from a nasty blow. While Gould knelt to check the officer was alive, Evans opened the fire-exit door and burst outside. There he was, standing against the railing, preparing to leap over. At last she had him.

With an effort, Mason raised his hands and put them behind his head. He heard the woman approach and pat him down.

'What the hell are you carrying?' She removed his guns, dropped them to the ground and kicked them away.

'I was hunting a wild animal. I needed all the help I could get.' He continued staring at the church opposite, seeing one, then two more people dash out screaming, the sounds all but lost in the traffic noise.

Evans clearly hadn't noticed. 'Wild animal, eh? Yeah, I've been tracking a wild animal myself.'

'Not like this one.'

'Oh, you'd be surprised.' Evans pulled him round to face her. She'd studied the photograph of Harry Moore, and this wasn't him.

'Who the hell are you?'

'Ralph Mason,' he replied. 'And you?'

'Janice Evans, Metropolitan Police. So you're Mason . . . Moore was at your place earlier. Why was he looking for you? And where the hell is he now?'

'Well,' Mason began. 'Answering the first question could take a while, so I'll skip to the second.' He turned and pointed to the church. 'He's in there. But you need to understand something before you go in after him.'

Gould had appeared from the fire exit as Evans approached with Mason. He helped her escort the man to the front of the gallery.

'OK,' she said. 'Go and put him in the car. I'm going

to check out the church.' She saw Lockhart marching towards them. 'Oh God, here we go . . .'

'Evans,' he began.

'It's Detective Inspector Evans, for your information.'

'Sorry, but I just heard our man has gone into the church.'

'I know. I'm going there now. Gould . . .' She handed Mason over.

'No!' Mason struggled. 'Please, you have to listen to me, that man is—' Just then he caught sight of Gerontius and Leah. They were being held back from the front of the gallery by officers. 'Please let me explain. You can't just go in and get him. You don't know who he is.'

'Yes we do. His name's Harry Moore; he should have died in a car crash—'

'He's also . . .' Mason lowered his voice so only Evans and Gould could hear him. 'He's also the father of that boy over there,' he said, pointing to Gerontius. Evans looked, then turned back to Mason, who added: 'And if he finds out his dad isn't really eight years dead but the very thing that's been trying to kill us all day, it could destroy him.'

Evans tried to decide quickly if Mason was telling the truth or not. 'DS Lockhart, do me a favour and go and take that boy's details. We'll be over by the church . . . Jesus, why can't I get an easy case once in a while?'

Evans, Gould and Mason headed back to the church of St Martin-in-the-Fields, leaving a baffled Lockhart rummaging in his coat for his pocket book and pen.

* * *

When Lockhart had finished questioning Gerontius, he rushed back over to the trio standing before the church. His expression made it quite clear that he was used to being in charge of things, not taking orders from some stranger.

'Look at this mess! We have to get this traffic flowing again,' he shouted over the din of horns and confused shouts. He strode across to Evans, following her gaze up to the front doors of the church.

'What's the boy's name?'

She too stared at the doors, knowing she would have to go up there, but dreading it.

'Er . . . pretty weird name actually,' he said, checking his pocket book to be sure he was pronouncing it correctly. 'Gerontius Moore – born July—'

'Shit,' Evans said.

'It is him then,' Gould said, hardly believing it.

'Just my luck.'

'Look, my guys can't hold the traffic back for ever. I've got to get—'

'I know,' Evans replied. 'But not until we've cleared this place. You've no idea what's in there.'

'Well, perhaps I should go in and find out.'

'I wouldn't do that. He's very dangerous. We need to wait for the armed officers.'

'You can wait for them if you like,' Lockhart said gruffly. 'I'm going in.'

'No!' Evans moved to stop him as a blood-curdling scream issued from the church.

'God,' Mason said, 'what the hell's going on in there?'

* * *

Haller's muscles no longer felt solid, they were just bags of limp tissue; distorted, squashed out of shape. As the world began to slip away from him, he cast his mind back to the day when everything changed. The day he stopped being Harry Moore, the husband and father, and became Haller, the outcast, the monster . . .

25: TOMB OF THE HAMRAMMR

Waking up was like being dragged through a thorn bush naked. Pain consumed his body like a holy fire. He opened his eyes and saw red clouds, or clouds that looked red because of the film of blood that coated his vision. The stinging sensation in his left cheek alternated between hot and cold, as air was sucked in through the holes in the burning, exposed flesh left by the creature's teeth. He'd been badly mauled, and yet was still alive. He looked to his right, and saw, for the first time, the horror that was left of his wife, the woman he had loved for nearly two decades. He couldn't breathe. What could possibly have done this to them? What could have torn their lives apart so utterly in the space of minutes? And then the answer was revealed. It crept into view from behind a clump of trees, then moved slowly towards the car on all fours as it approached what looked like a small body lying in the snow. It was a body Harry Moore knew only too well.

No! Anger boiled inside him like never before. He tried to move, but was almost paralysed. The creature was sniffing the body of the unconscious child now, deciding, perhaps, which bit to eat first. The anger that consumed Harry Moore now turned to fury, bolstered by the scorching agony that consumed him.

But the pain wasn't right. Surely it shouldn't have burned so much? Unless it was a reaction to the temperature, or to the shock. With an enormous effort he was able to raise his left arm. There were deep gouges along its length, and his shirt had been shredded in the frenzy of the attack. But what the hell was happening? Steam wasn't merely rising but hissing from the wounds as they ... closed up. The flesh was knitting together before his very eyes, as though each second was a day, a week. He must be delirious, hallucinating ... or dreaming perhaps? In no time at all he was looking at an arm completely untouched by any physical violence – in fact, almost unblemished. The rest of his body felt better too. He could move his legs now, and his back. Then, almost as soon as the agony had departed, a new sensation gripped him.

It began in his chest. His ribs ballooned outwards in one swift motion, making him sit up. He vomited on the damp ground between his legs, as his body shook uncontrollably. His neck twitched and expanded. He moved onto his knees, then his feet extended, pushing his whole weight upwards. His toenails and fingernails were thickening, hardening and curling into claws. He felt a scream rising in his throat, but when he released it, it was more of a low, prolonged yawn. Even as his jaws began to burn and extend outwards from his face, all he could think was: *What the hell is happening to me?* He wasn't dreaming, that was beyond doubt, so perhaps he was in hell.

Gazing into the night sky, he prayed for deliverance. His whole body was exploding in slow motion, each appendage warping with excruciating purpose. His shirt tore, then his trousers, as every part of him morphed into something new. He spat blood, then felt his ears grow and taper to points. His jaws now stopped moving and he could see that a soft grey fur covered them, along with what looked like whiskers, growing from the muzzle like an accelerated grass. He dropped onto all fours. Something stabbed through his skin from the inside and he felt cool air just above his backside. Something was moving there. It was a tail, black-tipped and bushy.

He licked his tongue around the new jaws. He realized with new-found shock that his mouth was again full of blood and strange stone-like objects. He coughed and spat the teeth onto the ground before him as new incisors and canines took their place. These teeth were foreign, sharp, and stabbed his tongue every time it went near them.

Oh God, please stop this, please stop this from happening. His jaws clamped together, the new teeth grinding against one another. With a final twitch of the neck, his body stopped changing. For some moments he waited, panting, wondering if the awesome attack on his body would resume; then, sensing it was over, he stood up.

His chest bloomed with a huge breath of air. He exhaled and felt every muscle in his new body scream from the stress of rebirth. He ran his hands all over his head, his neck, shoulders and chest, understanding the shape he now took. The creature hadn't killed him after all. It had done something far worse. Looking up, snorting air through his nostrils and gritting his teeth, he glared at his attacker, still inspecting the small body on the ground.

'Yuhhhh,' he roared, confused that he was no longer able to form words properly. 'You!' That was better, and this time the monster looked up and saw him, tensing itself, ready to pounce. But Harry Moore wasn't scared any more. He strode over to it, the rags of his torn clothes blowing in the cold breeze. Then he broke into a run.

They both leaped into the air at the same time, their bodies crashing together, then slamming to the ground, claws flailing, teeth gnashing. Harry raked the other creature's chest, then bit into its jaw, blood spraying everywhere, turning the snow pink. The other beast howled its anguish, then punched Harry in the chest, drawing blood and removing his grip. They separated and circled each other, blood dripping from wounds that were healing faster than Harry could believe possible. The pain was augmenting his fury, making him more and more eager to tear his enemy apart. He turned and once more gazed upon the ruined body of the only woman he'd ever loved. He heard the beast running towards him so he reached out and grasped something in his left paw. As his enemy was about to land on his back, he whirled round and swung the heavy branch at its head, sending it reeling away into the snow, dazed. Without hesitation he followed it and began pummelling the beast's head with the branch until the skull opened. He only ceased his frenzied attack when the branch broke in half. The body had changed back into its human form now, and the injuries hadn't healed. The head was a mess. As Harry stared at the man the beast had once been, he too changed back, then fell to his knees, crying openly, unleashing his hurt, his loss.

When he was able to think straight, he got up and walked solemnly over to his son. Gerontius lay still, only his stomach moving up and down, the breath issuing like smoke from his mouth. He picked up the small body and placed it carefully back inside the car. Harry knew his own life was as good as over. The life he'd had up until that point at least. He couldn't go back now. He'd seen werewolf movies. Whether they were accurate or not, he knew it was too much of a risk to try and remain a father. The possibilities were horrifying. He would learn to control what he was; perhaps try to turn it into something positive. And if he couldn't . . . then he would end it. He had to disappear, no matter how utterly heart-rending that would prove. He sat by the car, thinking. He would contact the emergency services. But when they arrived, they would wonder where he had gone, and whose body lay with its head smashed open, unless . . . Of course.

All at once the way ahead was clear, as though it had been preordained. He quickly took off his clothes, shivering as his skin was exposed to the terrible cold. He dressed the corpse, then laid it beside the body of his wife, trying all the while not to look at her. When he'd finished, he looked at the body. It might just work, but the face . . . He had no idea if Gerontius or anyone else would have to identify the body. If they did, they'd see it wasn't him. The face was a mess, but not enough to make it unrecognizable. He tried to change again, but couldn't do it. Just thinking about it didn't seem to be enough. Then he remembered how angry he'd been and the prickly sensation returned.

When he was the beast once more, he raked the corpse's face until it was no longer human. The task was nowhere near as awful or as sickening as he'd expected, but just as he finished, he heard a vehicle stop by the roadside above. A door slammed and there were voices. He turned and bounded into the trees, not knowing where he was going, or what he intended to do, just wanting to be as far away from that appalling scene as possible. As he darted through the undergrowth into ever-blackening forest, he prayed it would work. He prayed no one would guess what had happened. He prayed Gerontius would never know his father's true fate. But now, as he lay dying on the floor of the church, it was quite clear that he hadn't prayed hard enough.

The ceiling of St Martin-in-the-Fields was the last beautiful thing he would gaze upon. He coughed up something horrible and rolled onto his side. *Please*, he thought. *Oh God, please, don't let him see me. Don't let him ever know . . . Oh, son . . . It wasn't me . . .* Tears bled from his eyes now. Regret, guilt, bitterness and a deep love that had been buried for too long swathed him. *I love you so much, Gerry . . . It wasn't me . . .*

More police officers had been diverted from the gallery to the road around the church, so people were now escaping the temporary cordon the police had set up at the top of the square. The children dodged their way through several constables and ran to the small group outside the church. A frustrated Gerontius demanded that Evans let Mason go with them.

'Whoa. Excuse me, young man, you're in my way,' she said, trying to move round him. 'And you shouldn't be here.' She didn't know what to do. This was the beast's son. What if it chose this moment to come back outside and change back into its human form?

'You don't understand. He helped us,' Gerontius insisted, indicating Mason.

'He saved our lives,' Leah added. 'He saved us from that thing.'

Evans hesitated a moment, sharing a look with Gould. 'Is this true?' she asked Mason. He nodded.

'Yes, well, I'm sorry, but until I've questioned him, I'm not letting him out of my sight. Now you really need to get back away from here. If you like I can get an officer to drive you home. We can talk about the whole matter tomorrow. Gould, take them back to the square and get someone to give them a lift.'

'Sure.'

'Don't worry,' Mason said to Gerontius as he and Leah were escorted away towards the flashing lights of the squad cars. 'I'll be fine . . . Just got a bit of explaining to do.'

'It'll be all right,' Evans added. 'We'll deal with it. You've nothing to worry about any more.'

Gerontius resisted Gould's urging to move away. Leah sympathized with the look of exasperation on his face.

'That's it,' Lockhart suddenly announced. 'I'm sick of waiting.' He called to two other officers standing nearby and they ran up the steps of the church.

'Shit! Gould, hold him.' She gave Mason back to her

partner, pulled out her gun and followed Lockhart into the building.

'I'll be all right, I promise,' Mason said, trying to ease Gerontius's fears. 'They can't exactly arrest me for trying to kill a werewolf, can they? As long as they don't find out about my previous escapades, I'll be fine.'

Just then Evans reappeared at the top of the steps to the church, an even more baffled Lockhart appearing behind her.

'It's OK,' she called down to them. 'It's dead.'

Lockhart gave her a strange look, then issued orders to his officers not to let anyone inside the building. He followed Evans down the steps to the street.

'Gould,' Evans said, 'get those kids home. Now!'

'Yes, ma'am.'

'But . . . Mason,' Gerontius said, not wanting to go. 'It's not fair.'

'He'll be fine, Gerry,' Leah said. 'They'll realize he was only doing what anyone else would have done. Your dad would have done the same if he was here. Come on.'

Evans escorted Mason away from the church, in the same direction as Gould and the children.

'Don't worry, I'll arrange it so the body is buried in his father's grave, where it belongs. This whole thing will be brushed under the carpet. No one would believe a word of it anyway.'

'If he ever found out . . .' Mason began.

'I know, I know. Poor kid.'

*   *   *

236

As they walked away from Mason, and the end of the madness, Gerontius knew that Leah was right. He remembered his father the last time he'd seen him alive, struggling with all his might to keep the car on the road, staring into the eyes of that evil, hungry beast. If he had been here, he would have done exactly the same thing as Mason. There was no doubt about that. That's the kind of man he was.

26: BREAKING THE LAW

Slaughter emptied the glass of rum and took it into the kitchen, where he stood for a moment, sucking his teeth, deliberating the pros and cons of a third glass. It was a warm night for the time of year, and too much rum gave him a terrible morning-after headache. He abandoned the glass on the draining board and went to the back door. It was locked, just as it should be. He'd taught the whole family – wife, son and daughter – to treat the house like a fortress. Something that was even more important now after Haller's visit. The nerve of the man!

He unlocked the door and stepped out into the garden. He could hear the loud music playing in his daughter's room upstairs. *The sooner she gets a social life the better,* he thought. He could also hear traffic and the distant drone of a plane passing overhead. He reached into his shirt pocket for his packet of cigars, but they weren't there. *Damn.* He'd forgotten to buy more on the way home from work. He blew out a long deep breath of dissatisfaction. Maybe another glass of rum would take his mind off it. Suddenly the volume of the music in the room upstairs increased. *That bloody girl!* He turned back to the house, but before he reached the door a voice stopped him.

'Slaughter . . .' He recognized it, but it was different. No longer full of the joviality of youth. It was the voice of someone who'd changed a lot in the last few hours. Ordinarily Slaughter wouldn't have felt intimidated in the slightest: if anything he'd have been angry at the thought of someone trespassing on his property. But something was very wrong here. He turned round, trying not to look bothered, ready to intimidate the intruder into submission. Instead, when he saw the man standing only a metre or two away, he froze. He was as he remembered, only his clothes were torn and bloodied, and his eyes . . . Something about them was wrong. It wasn't just the hunger, the malice in them, but something else, something . . . feral.

'I know what you did,' Cain said, nodding.

'What . . . ? What are you talking about?' Slaughter was almost mesmerized. The man's eyes seemed to be glowing yellow.

'You sent that thing after us. You sent it to kill us.'

'I don't know—'

'Didn't quite finish the job though, did it? As you can see. And now I have to suffer what it's done to me.'

'*It?* What do you mean *it?*'

'Don't tell me you don't know.'

'Don't know what?'

'My God . . .' Cain stared into Slaughter's eyes. 'You really have no idea . . .'

'No idea of what?' Slaughter backed away towards the house, praying that something or someone would intervene to disrupt this awkward, disturbing situation.

240

Cain started laughing, a deep, throaty sound that Slaughter didn't like one bit. 'Oh, you're going to love this, Ray. You're really going to love it.'

And then the impossible happened. Cain's face started moving outwards on its own. Hair formed in places it shouldn't. Snapping sounds accompanied the moving and buckling of bones, and a horrible breath plumed out as organs shifted, muscles broke down and re-formed and teeth fell out and were replaced. Slaughter was about to scream as the monster lunged forward and took him in its crushing, bleeding embrace.

A few minutes later, when Mrs Slaughter went outside to find out where her husband had disappeared to, she was confronted by a scene from an abattoir. Blood had soaked the wall and patio, turning the surfaces black in the darkness. Her husband's body was halfway across the lawn, horribly mauled. She screamed and ran over to the remains of the man she loved, stopping when she realized the body had no head. The second scream caught in her throat. Turning slowly, she spotted the missing object . . .

It was sitting in the bird bath, mouth wide open, staring straight at her. Four deep claw marks from some awful beast had torn open its forehead.

Author's Note

Canis Lupus

Someone I know once described the werewolf myth as the product of a 'deranged imagination', and he was right. The werewolf, wulver, lycanthrope – call it what you will – is nothing but pure fantasy. But in film and literature it remains an exciting device, feeding on the part of us that is terrified not only by slavering, hairy beasts, but also by the intrusion of disease, possession. When I was a boy, what terrified me most about the idea of the werewolf was not meeting one, but actually becoming one. The loss of control and of self is a terrifying prospect, not to mention the guilt of killing innocent victims on a moonlit lycanthropic spree.

But while the werewolf can be entertaining and exciting, it is important to remember that we all have a responsibility to the wolf itself, which has been given a 'big, bad' name.

The myth of the werewolf has long been a part of human culture, with its origin in the myths surrounding the wolf itself. For a long time the wolf instilled fear in people all over Europe, and then in America when the early settlers arrived. But rather than being a malign presence itself, the wolf is more a victim of man's ignorance and willingness to believe the wild and fanciful tales of scaremongers. In many cases wolves were used as an excuse for livestock losses, a scapegoat to cover up the crimes of human neighbours.

But regardless of the uneasy relationship that the wolf shares with man, it is a beautiful animal, with just as much right to a place in nature as any other. The wolf was seen as a very spiritual creature by the Native Americans, and treated as a 'brother'. If only everyone had embraced this vision.

It is also worth remembering that domestic dogs are descended from the wolf: prehistoric man tamed them and brought them into his society long ago. In a way, the wolf has been among us throughout history, and perhaps it is time that it is given more respect.

Dean Carter

The Hand of the Devil

by

DEAN VINCENT CARTER

When Ashley Reeves, a young journalist working
for freak-of-nature magazine *Missing Link*, receives
a letter promising him the story of his life, his life
is exactly what it might cost him.

The letter is from Reginald Mather, who at
first seems no more than an eccentric collector of
insects, happy to live in isolation on a remote island.
But when Reeves finds himself stranded with Mather and
unearths the horrific truth behind his past, he is thrown
headlong into a macabre nightmare that quickly
spirals out of control. His life is in danger . . .
and Mather is not his only enemy . . .

ISBN: 978 0 552 55297 4

The Fearful

by

KEITH GRAY

For those who want to believe, no proof is needed.
But for those who can't believe, no evidence is enough.

The legend says that in 1699, schoolteacher
William Milmullen and his five pupils visited Lake Mou,
but only William returned. He claimed that a terrifying
creature had risen from the lake and devoured the boys.
But had it? And if it all happened so long ago, does
it really matter to anyone nowadays anyway?

The legacy of that tragedy lives on in the town
of Moutonby. A town divided between those who
believe that something terrible still lurks deep
down in the lake, and those who don't.

Tim Milmullen wishes he knew. Every day
he watches the dark water, looking for a sign.
Because if the stories are true, if 'the dragon' in the
lake is real, then according to the legend he's the
only one who can stop it from killing again.

ISBN: 978 0 099 45656 8

THE SPOOK'S APPRENTICE

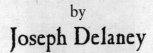

by

Joseph Delaney

'The Spook's trained many, but precious few completed their time,' Mam said, 'and those that did aren't a patch on him. They're flawed or weak or cowardly. They walk a twisted path taking money for accomplishing little. So there's only you left now, son. You're the last chance. The last hope. Someone has to do it. Someone has to stand against the dark. And you're the only one who can.'

Thomas Ward is the seventh son of a seventh son and has been apprenticed to the local Spook. The job is hard, the Spook is distant and many apprentices have failed before him. Somehow Thomas must learn how to exorcize ghosts, contain witches and bind boggarts. But when he is tricked into freeing Mother Malkin, the most evil witch in the County, the horror begins . . .

ISBN: 978 0 099 45645 2

The Devil's Footsteps
by
E. E. RICHARDSON

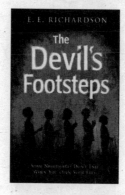

It was just a bit of fun, a local legend.
The Devil's Footsteps: thirteen stepping stones,
and whichever one you stopped on in the rhyme
could predict how you would die. A harmless game
for kids – and nobody ever died from a game.

But it's not a game to Bryan. He's seen the Dark
Man, because the Dark Man took his brother five years
ago. He's tried to tell himself that it was his imagination,
that the Devil's Footsteps are just stones and the Dark
Man didn't take Adam. But Adam's still gone.

And then Bryan meets two other boys who have
their own unsolved mysteries. Someone or something is
after the children in the town. And it all comes back to
the rhyme that every local child knows by heart:

Thirteen steps to the Dark Man's door,
Won't be turning back no more . . .

ISBN: 978 0 552 55171 7